5

"Into the bed, Virginia."

Dillon came to his feet and braced himself for the newest confrontation.

Virginia faltered and her beautiful eyes widened. As usual, her chin went into the air and her shoulders squared. "What are you going to do?"

Gently he said, "I told you I'd have to tie you, remember?"

"You're not going to tie me, Dillon."

The warning was there, but the trembling in her tone belied the vehemence of her words. He felt like an animal, and he hated himself, hated what he had to do. "There's only one other choice."

Hope shone in her eyes, mixed with the caution she tried so hard to hide. "What choice?"

"I'll have to sleep with you." He stared at her, refusing to back down from the accusation on her face, refusing to acknowledge the stirring of lust that twisted his gut and tightened his groin.

"I'll have to sleep with you...all night long."

Dear Reader,

I'm often asked where I get my ideas. Well, I get them from *you,* from observing people I meet or see. And from music and art and movies—I suppose just from the world around me, and from enjoying life. *Taken!,* my all-time favorite book, was conceived while in the car listening to a Billy Joel song about a woman called Virginia. It took only a few lines to get my mind racing.

Taken! will always have a special place in my heart. Dillon is every woman's dream, so how could I not adore him? And in response to your letters, I've made this the most sensual book yet. Keep the letters coming, and thank you for making 1998 such a wonderful year for me.

Lori Foster

Romance that burns out of control!

Don't miss the next red-hot reads from Temptation's BLAZE:

#704 A TOUCH OF BLACK VELVET (Oct. '98)
Carrie Alexander

#708 FLIRTING WITH DANGER (Nov. '98)
Jamie Denton

#715 TANTALIZING (Jan. '99)
Lori Foster

TAKEN!
Lori Foster

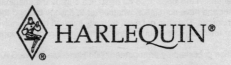

HARLEQUIN®

TORONTO • NEW YORK • LONDON
AMSTERDAM • PARIS • SYDNEY • HAMBURG
STOCKHOLM • ATHENS • TOKYO • MILAN • MADRID
PRAGUE • WARSAW • BUDAPEST • AUCKLAND

To Cheryl Hopewell, for so many things; wonderful
friendship, incredible support and for being a good
listener when I need to talk. You've been there when I
didn't expect it, and when I needed it most.
Thank you so very, very much.

ISBN 0-373-25798-8

TAKEN!

Copyright © 1998 by Lori Foster.

1

THE HEAT SWELLED within him until he thought he'd explode with lust. This wasn't what he'd expected, wasn't what he'd planned on. Her nipple stiffened under the gentle abrasion of his rough fingertips and Virginia groaned, thrilling him, turning him inside out with need. She twined her fingers in his hair and said with a touch of desperation, "Please."

Dillon felt the silky smooth, pliant flesh of her breast, heard her choppy breathing and soft plea, and he forgot his purpose. He forgot that he had ulterior motives, that he wasn't actually attracted to this woman.

"Dillon…"

"Shh. It's all right, honey." And it was, better than all right. It was incredible.

He pushed her coat farther out of his way and shoved her blouse higher. Her breast, full and firm and heavy, nestled against his palm, and more than anything, he wanted her naked. He wanted to see the color of her nipples by the scant moonlight coming through the windshield, to see the pleasure in her exotic hazel eyes, eyes that were usually hard with determination and arrogance but now were soft with pleasure and desire. For him.

He pressed open-mouth kisses to the smooth skin of her throat and breathed in her unique scent. He'd never noticed before that she had a unique scent. He'd never noticed how sexy she was, or imagined how hotly she would respond to his touch. She gasped and he whispered to her, soothing her as his fingers plucked at her nipple, rolling and teasing. As her entire body trembled with need, she moaned and he wanted to moan, too. This wasn't right, but it felt too damned right.

What had started out as necessary seduction now seemed amazingly like blind sexual need. There was no way he could deny his enjoyment of this little rendezvous, or the way his blood surged through his body to settle into an insistent throb in his groin. He was as hard as a stone, hurting with it, and Virginia was far too astute not to notice.

The car was cramped, but it didn't matter, and even though it was a miserably cold night, they were cozy, sharing the warmth of the heater and their combined sexual heat as the wind whistled around them. He knew that inside the mansion, the party was still going full blast. Lights shone from every window, sparkling across the snow-covered lawn, and the rumble of music drifted on the air. What he was doing, and where he was doing it, was dangerous, but he finally had her alone and he wasn't about to lose ground. He needed to push forward; too much time had been lost already.

For thirty-six years he'd been a mean, determined bastard—traits his father had instilled in him, insisted upon. He never forgot his purpose, never wavered from his course. Tonight, though, right this minute, he couldn't seem to force the plan to remain uppermost in his mind.

He wanted Virginia lying naked on the narrow seat, wanted to fit himself between her soft plump thighs and slide deep, deep inside her. He wanted to ride her hard until she made those sweet little sounds again, until she begged him to give her what she needed.

"Dillon, wait."

Her tone wasn't authoritative now. It didn't carry the sharp cut of command it normally did. Instead, her voice was low, overcome with need, and purely feminine. As a man, he relished the thought of proper balance with this particular woman who didn't act the way he expected a woman to act, the way he needed her to act.

She whispered his name again, and when he ignored her, she tightened her strong fingers in his hair. Taking her reaction as one of encouragement, he worked her bra aside, nuzzling with his lips. Her breasts were extremely sensitive, and he liked that. He imagined how it would be to make love to her, to find all her sensitive places with his hands, his mouth, his tongue and teeth. He wanted to taste her, to draw her deep into the heat of his mouth, to suck her gently and then, not so gently, devour her.

He smoothed a hand over her soft, slightly rounded belly and heard her sharp groan. He needed to touch her, all of her. His fingers pressed lower, slipping between her thighs, seeking, probing, feeling the throbbing heat.

Suddenly, she jerked away. "Dillon, no."

He heard her gasping, heard the trembling in her tone. She pressed her head back against the seat and closed her eyes.

"I'm sorry. I can't do this."

Reality started to nudge his lust-fogged brain. *She* couldn't do this? He was the one who'd been forcing himself for the sake of his plan—at first. His sole purpose in coming to Delaport City, Ohio, had been to seduce her, and in the process gain answers. Reluctance was in no way the proper response from her to his lovemaking. In fact, it was so far out of line with his original intention that he scowled. "Virginia..."

"No," she said, shaking her head. "No, this isn't right. Hiding out here with you as if I'm ashamed. I shouldn't treat you so shabbily. Just because you work for the company and I have the authority to fire you doesn't give me the right to treat you with less than full respect."

As she spoke, her voice gathered strength and she straightened her silk blouse, pulling it down over her breasts. He tried his damnedest to catch a glimpse of that taunting nipple he'd wanted so badly to taste.

Then it sank in. She thought she was treating him badly because they were sneaking? They *had* to sneak, or his plan would never work.

He cupped her cheek. Long curls of titian hair had escaped their pins and now hung over her rounded shoulders. Those curls surprised him. Usually her hair was pulled up and tidy and he'd had no idea how long it was. Loose, it made her look almost vulnerable—not that anyone would ever think of Virginia Johnson in such human terms. It also made her seem very feminine. He toyed with a loose strand and it was incredibly soft against his fingertips. He wondered what she'd look like with it completely undone. That red hair of hers would frame her white body perfectly, maybe curl around her lush breasts, giving her an earthy, pagan appearance.

He shook his head at his meandering thoughts. He must have been too long without a woman, but then, he'd had other priorities lately. Namely, saving his brother's ass. He had to get a grip, had to remember the purpose of this little seduction.

He summoned up his most bland tone, the one he knew she wanted and expected from subordinates. "It's all right, Virginia. You can't be seen with me and we both know it. Cliff would be outraged and your reputation might be ruined."

She shook that stubborn head of hers. In the two weeks he'd spent cautiously wooing her, he'd learned Virginia Johnson had stubbornness down to a fine, irritating art, along with arrogance and a complete lack of business modesty. She knew she was good at making corporate decisions and she wanted everyone else to know it, too, even if she had to shove the fact down people's throats.

"I don't care what my brother thinks. He's a snob and we seldom get along anyway. He doesn't own me and he has no say over how I live my life."

"That's not the impression he gives." Dillon knew he had to speak carefully so he didn't give

himself away. Deferring to anyone wasn't cus-
tomary for him. He led his life in a unique fashion, following rules of his own making. He lived
by a code of honor that was independent of the
strictures of society. Except for his father and his
brother, Dillon owed nothing to anyone. But Virginia was a bossy, powerful woman, damn her,
and as used to calling the shots as he. He cleared
his throat. "Your brother is very protective."

"Ha! He's a bully and I'm the only one with
the guts to stand up to him, because I control the
majority of the money. Cliff knows that without
me, he'd destroy the company in a matter of
weeks."

Even in the darkness he could see the ire on
her face. She wasn't exactly pretty—at least, he'd
never thought so before—and she was entirely
too headstrong and self-contained. She enjoyed
giving orders to everyone in her realm. She was
also a bit too plump. Only, she hadn't felt too
plump against him a minute ago. She'd felt soft
and warm and comfortably rounded. He
frowned at himself. "Virginia, I can't let you—"

"Can't let me?" she interrupted, one thin auburn brow climbing high as she met his gaze.
"You can't stop me, Dillon. I always do as I
please—you know that." With efficient movements, she rebuttoned her coat and started to
open the door.

He caught her arm. From the minute he'd first
forced an introduction, he'd damn near bitten
holes in his tongue to keep from revealing his
true nature. Sometimes the urge to put her in her

place, wherever that might be, almost overwhelmed him.

She glared down at where his hand circled her arm, then slowly raised those incredible eyes to his in a look that plainly said, *You dare?*

The little witch might have the hots for him, but she didn't want anyone telling her what to do, which probably accounted as much for her matronly status as did her excess weight and unremarkable features. Most of the men who worked for her steered clear because she frightened them half to death and they weren't willing to put their careers on the line. The rest simply weren't interested.

Dillon wasn't worried about his career. Working for the company was only a temporary sham, his way of getting close to her so that he could ultimately ruin her brother's destructive plans. But even if that hadn't been true, he would never have let a woman, any woman, dictate to him. There were easier ways to make a living than bowing under to the tyrannical rule of an iron maiden.

"Sweetheart, listen to me." He turned his secure hold into a caress to pacify her, and to some degree it worked. The only way he'd been able to get close to her had been to seduce her into wanting him. And seducing an iron maiden was no easy feat. He'd nearly depleted his store of ploys with her and he wasn't used to that. Women usually came to him easily enough, but Virginia had been so damn elusive his ego had taken a beating. Now the plan was more than a necessity; it was a personal challenge.

He'd finally been making headway, and then this. "Virginia, if you won't think of your own reputation, think of mine. If Cliff finds out about us, he'll fire me in a heartbeat. Is that what you want?" He had to keep their relationship secret so that later no one would suspect him.

She patted his hand in her condescending fashion. "Don't worry. I won't let him fire you. I hold controlling interest in the company. I have ultimate say over who goes and who stays."

He sighed, deliberately appearing put-upon. "I'm sorry, honey, but I won't have it. I'd look like a fool if I let a woman, any woman, defend me. People would start saying I was only after your money and—"

She waved a hand. "Nonsense. Everyone knows I'm never marrying, and that's the only way you could possibly get your hands on my money. We'd just be having an affair."

"Which is nobody's business but our own."

She frowned and he quickly retrenched, pulling together his frayed temper and gathering the remnants of his control. Why did she have to be so damn argumentative?

"I'm sorry," he said through gritted teeth, then managed to summon a calmer tone. "I didn't mean to yell at you. But what's between us is private. I want to keep it that way."

She still looked skeptical and he silently cursed her, while on the outside he did his best to appear hopeful. The damn shrew. What was it with this woman that she thought she had to control everyone and everything? Of course, he felt the same way, but it was different for him.

He'd been raised to be cautious, to take control and guide the events in his life. His father's renegade life-style had carried over into parenting, and every survival value had been passed on. Dillon accepted his right to control as a means to protect those around him. It was what he was used to, the way he understood life.

Virginia had led a pampered existence, so she had no excuse.

Finally, she nodded. "Oh, all right, if you're going to be that sensitive about it, I'll keep our...association private. But I'm not going to make love in a car. It's ridiculous."

"Of course not." This was the opening he'd been waiting for, a culmination of two weeks' work and endless, nerve-stretching patience. "But we could take a day off, go somewhere private and indulge ourselves." He swallowed, then forced himself to say, "I want you so bad, honey."

Now that he wasn't kissing and touching her, only listening to the grating, overbearing tone of her voice, all lust had died and he was once again filled with cold deliberation. She would be a pawn in the scheme of things, used and deceived so he could accomplish his goals, but he had no intention of making Virginia a victim. Though she might end up slightly humiliated, he wouldn't hurt her. He would go only as far as necessary to stop her brother and save his own.

True to her nature, she was already shaking her head no. "I can't take any time off right now. Too much to do. Just come to my home tonight. We'll leave separately so no one will know, seeing as how your reputation is so important to you."

He wanted to smack her for using that sneering tone. Obviously, she wanted just an hour or two with him, a quick toss in the hay, not the commitment of an entire evening. Although it was foolish, he felt very insulted; she might as well have labeled him a stud for hire. His male dignity was sorely tried.

He needed enough time to gain her trust and find the clues to the deception that threatened to destroy his brother. But he couldn't do that if Virginia's brother found out they were seeing each other. He answered her honestly. "No. It's too risky. Someone might see me at your place."

She heaved a dramatic sigh and glared at him, her hazel eyes appearing gold in the dark night. "Are you sure you really want to do this? I mean, for a man who only a few moments ago was in the throes of lust, you're setting up an awful lot of obstacles. I've never known anyone so ridiculously sensitive or so overly cautious."

Through narrowed eyes he searched her face, not quite sure how to answer her and keep the peace at the same time. Though her brother stood as a figurehead, it was Virginia who actually ran things. She was the only hope his brother had out of this damn mess.

She sighed again and said, "I'm sorry. That was uncalled for. To be honest, I'm not quite used to this."

He could believe that. What man would pursue a dragon lady? When he'd been kissing her and she'd been soft and pliant and feminine, he'd forgotten how cold and domineering she really was. But what he'd learned of her other side had been accidental. Not many men had ever tried to get past the brambles to see what lay beneath. If it hadn't been for Wade, he certainly wouldn't have tried. That thought bothered him and he shied away from it.

"Virginia, I know this is complicated, but I don't see any other way...."

"Maybe we should just forget the whole thing. I'm not exactly cut out for affairs and it's getting entirely too awkward."

"No!" Damn it, he couldn't waste time backtracking now. Getting her this far had taken longer than he'd expected. But here she was, lifting that damn supercilious eyebrow at his tone. He cleared his throat and had to clench his hands to keep from shaking her.

"What I meant," he said, painfully cajoling, "is that you can't change your mind on me. I need you too much." For good measure he kissed her again—then immediately forgot it was just for good measure and started enjoying himself. Her lips parted. Her tongue touched his.

Damn, but for a dragon lady she tasted fine— hot and sweet and sexy. Without making a conscious decision, he lifted his hand to that heavy breast again. Even through her sweater and coat, he could feel the softness of her as he kneaded her flesh. She moaned, and when he lifted his mouth from hers she whispered shakily, "Let me see what I can work out. I'll get in touch with you later in the week."

She had the door open before he could stop

her, but it was just as well. The driveway was packed with cars and they could have been caught by anyone coming or going. He'd gotten so wrapped up in the job at hand he'd been careless.

No one knew who he really was and he had to keep it that way, because once he gained Virginia's confidence and ruined her brother's plans, Dillon would disappear. If anyone suspected him of having a relationship with Virginia, he'd fail. And his brother, Wade, would be the one to suffer.

2

WHEN VIRGINIA STEPPED back into the mansion, entering through the kitchen door, she ran smack into her brother, Cliff. He looked at her suspiciously.

"What were you doing outside?"

She pushed him out of her way and pulled off her coat. All that kissing and touching had her overheated. She'd rebuttoned the coat only as a sort of barrier, a way to shield herself from the overwhelming attraction and confusing emotions Dillon made her feel. Being so strongly drawn to a man wasn't something she was used to. And especially not a man like Dillon. She shivered in memory. "I was indulging in a secret liaison, of course."

"Ha, ha. Very funny." With his tone as bland as an angry brother could manage, Cliff glared at her. "Like any man would be foolish enough to tangle with you."

Virginia just shook her head. In one respect, Cliff was right. Men rarely pursued her—at least, not men who only wanted to have a heated affair. The term *sex symbol* had never been used to describe her, not with her excess weight and incisive personality. Men who wanted to try to marry her for her company connections showed up by the dozen each year, but their intentions were far from honorable or complimentary, which partially accounted for her ruthlessness. She'd decided to stay single because she couldn't find a man who suited her—they were all either immoral money grubbers or complete wimps.

She'd had high hopes for Dillon when she first met him. Unlike the other fools Cliff invariably hired, Dillon stood apart. His body was long and hard and honed, not the type of physique achieved in a gym, but rather the kind that came from hard work day in and day out, over a lifetime. With broad shoulders and thick thighs, he looked more than capable of taking on any physical task. And he wore a certain confidence, as if he possessed an alertness unknown to most men.

He had the kind of intensity that made a woman feel surrounded and closed in. It didn't threaten her—nothing did. She'd grown up a chubby, unattractive middle child who'd had to learn to fight for everything she wanted, including affection. She'd forced her way into the business and into her father's trust. After living through her parents' deaths and the battles for power that followed, she knew that very little in life had the ability to alarm her, including Dillon's pursuit.

Unhappily, Dillon was proving to be something of a pushover, just like the others. One little word from her, and he tripped all over himself trying not to anger her. Why couldn't she find a man who could deal with her head-on?

She was disappointed by his lack of backbone, but not enough to call a halt to the affair. With any luck, Dillon might surprise her once he learned her bark was worse than her bite.

"Yoo-hoo, Virigina. Anyone home?" Cliff peered at her critically. "What are you up to that has you so distracted?"

Virginia sighed. "I'm not exactly in the mood right now for your prying or your sarcasm, Cliff. Shouldn't you be entertaining guests or something?"

"That's my line to you. We have important associates here tonight."

"Is that right? Such as your personal assistant? I saw Laura dutifully following you around earlier. In fact, she's probably looking for you right now."

Cliff stiffened. "Ms. Neil is no concern of yours."

In all honesty, Virginia really didn't care what Cliff did with his free time or his secretary, although she suspected he'd promoted Laura to personal assistant only as a way to get her in bed. In spite of her disapproval, it wasn't her business, so she just shrugged. "True enough. Now, what do you want, Cliff?"

"I want to know what you were doing outside that was so important you neglected your duties."

"We've been through this before, Brother." She kept her tone level, hoping to avoid a prolonged fight. She wanted to be alone so she could contemplate how to proceed with Dillon. "What I do with my life is none of your business. Stop pushing me or you won't like the consequences."

Just as she expected, Cliff fumed in impotent

silence and then stalked away. It was a shame
he'd been born first. It was a bigger shame her father had believed the company needed to be rep-
resented by a man, regardless of the fact that Cliff
was spineless and shallow and lacked the necessary business sense. Just because they dealt in
sporting equipment, her father felt a man would
be a more traditional head for the company.

Virginia would have done a much better job of
it. She'd learned the business from the sales floor
up, working part-time at their three mall locations while taking business courses and acting as
an apprentice at the main offices. She'd absorbed
every nuance of the business, and she thrived
there, but regardless of all she was capable of,
she wasn't male and that mattered most to her father. At least he'd had the foresight to leave her a
controlling interest. No, she wasn't the president,
and she didn't interfere overly in the daily running of the business, but no major decisions
could be made without her. And that one small
stipulation in her father's will had garnered her
near hate from Cliff.

Her brother had always been a petty child, and
he'd grown into a petty man. Still, they used to
be able to get along, to find a middle ground.
Now she hardly knew him—or her younger sister, Kelsey.

Kelsey also held a share of the company, but
she hated to get caught in the cross fire between
Virginia and Cliff, and usually gave her proxy to
one of the other voting board members. She
threw herself, instead, into her college studies

and her computers, taking great pains to separate herself from the family business.

There were times, like tonight, when Virginia wished she had the same options. It would have been nice to be just an ordinary woman for once. Any woman. Then she wouldn't have to question Dillon's motives in pursuing her.

He wanted her; she knew that. He couldn't have faked his reactions in the car. She'd been more than a little aware of his erection, heavy and full, pressing into her hip. But there was more to it than that, she was certain. And if it wasn't a part of the company he wanted, then what?

She'd read his file when Cliff had first hired him to oversee their security department, mostly because he didn't seem to be the typical Johnson's Sporting Goods employee. He didn't look as if he'd ever played a recreational sport in his life and every time he donned a tie, it seemed to choke him. No, with eyes so dark they almost appeared black, he looked more like a mercenary. Or a renegade. And his file had revealed that he'd never held a steady job for long. The man skipped around the country, and sometimes out of the country. It was for certain he'd been somewhere warm recently, because his skin was darkly tanned, contrasting sharply with the sandy brown hair that hung beyond his collar.

His qualifications and references had been excellent, plus he'd had some military training, so Cliff had hired him regardless of the way he looked.

Dillon knew his business. In the first few days

he'd instigated additional safeguards on several
levels, approved by Virginia, that would save the
company substantial funds in the long run. Ruthless in many ways, he'd already fired two night
guards, claiming that the men had been leaving
their posts, playing poker and not paying attention to their jobs. Dillon wouldn't allow any der-
eliction of duty. He now did a personal background check on everyone hired under his
jurisdiction, which encompassed all the company offices and the store locations, as well. He
took his responsibilities seriously and expected
the same of everyone else.

The intelligence in his dark eyes was easy to
read, as visible as his strength and every bit as
appealing. Even his disdain of her family's business seemed sexy to Virginia. But still, he was an
enigma.

She'd give him one night, she decided. Even if
he did prove later to be a swindler with ulterior
motives, it wouldn't matter. She'd never get
drawn in by a wimp, so there was no risk of a
bruised heart. She wanted a man who could
stand toe-to-toe with her, a man to be her partner
in life, who was her equal in every way.

But Dillon, with his incredible body and incredible kisses, would work nicely for now to fill
a terrible void. Her aching loneliness had lingered too long, and she needed a little attention,
the kind only a man could give a woman.

No, she could never get serious about a man
like him. But every woman had the right to a fantasy on occasion. And Dillon Jones was six feet

two inches of hard, throbbing fantasy material.
He'd do just fine.

THE MINUTE DILLON opened his door, Wade
pounced.

"What happened? How did it go?"

Damn, this was just what he needed. The entire night had been irritating enough; he didn't
need to be accosted by his brother right now.

He shrugged out of his battered leather coat
and kicked off his low boots. "What the hell are
you doing here? Are you trying to screw things
up?" If anyone found out they were related...

"I was careful," Wade protested, looking
wounded. "I took a bus to the corner and then
walked the rest of the way. Besides, it's dark. No
one could have seen me. Now, tell me what happened!"

His little brother, the personification of espio-
nage excellence. What a joke. They'd been raised
by different parents, and their upbringing and
their outlooks on life couldn't have been more
different. "Calm down, Wade," he said. "Nothing's happening yet. Hopefully, this coming
week sometime."

"Damn it!" Wade began to pace, his turmoil
the complete opposite of his usual, carefree light-
heartedness. "What is the matter with that
woman! No woman has ever treated you like
this. Usually you're the one forced to turn them
away."

Even though Wade's words echoed his own
earlier sentiments, Dillon shook his head. "Don't
be ridiculous. I'm no Romeo." Then he added

with a frown, "And Virginia is no fool." A virago, but not stupid.

"Ha! She's a stuck-up bit—"

"Shut up, Wade." His defense of Virginia took him by surprise. He was automatically protective of women, the trait inborn, but of all the women he'd ever known, Virginia was least in need of his chivalry. Still, he didn't like the idea of using her this way, even if there wasn't any choice. Virginia had the answers he needed, and there was only one way to get them.

Fuming, Wade finally dropped into an overstuffed chair. "It has to be soon, Dillon. We're running out of time and I can't take much more of this. I keep having visions of being locked away in prison."

"I told you it won't come to that. I won't let it. If nothing else, I'll get you out of the country before that happens. You could come home with me to Mexico until I get things straightened out." Then he added, just to distract Wade, "How's Kelsey holding up?"

"She's got morning sickness." Wade looked ready to sink into the depths of depression. "She's sick and that damn brother of hers isn't helping matters by doing his best to separate us. He thinks that since I'm without a job and accused of a crime Kelsey won't want me. She's afraid to see me, in case he has me locked up right now. I have to settle for the occasional phone call and it's intolerable. At this rate, she'll be giving birth before we have a chance to get married!"

Dillon went into the kitchen and opened a can

of cola, then began stripping off his shirt. For the sake of the party at the mansion and his scheme, he'd donned a dress shirt and tie. He hated ties. Wearing them to the office during the week was torture.

The lengths he went to for his brother.

Half brother, he corrected himself. They hadn't shared the same father, but Wade was still his brother in every sense of the word. Blood was blood, as his father had been fond of preaching. You didn't turn your back on a blood relative.

When their mother had died, leaving Wade alone, he'd made the effort to find Dillon, wanting him at the funeral, wanting to become a part of his life.

At the time, Dillon had just finished a stint in the military. He'd been living the life of a loner, independent of everyone, even his father, with no clue as to where his mother had gone or what she'd been doing, and not particularly interested in knowing. He certainly hadn't heard that she'd remarried and birthed another son. All his father had ever told him was that she hadn't wanted either of them, and that as soon as she could, she'd abandoned Dillon. She'd turned her back on both of them, and that said it all. They'd never talked about her; given the circumstances, it hadn't seemed necessary.

Women had come and gone in their lives while Dillon was growing up, but none of them had been all that important. His father's relationships never lasted; women were just a necessary convenience for him.

Though he and his father were close, Dillon

had never really understood his attitudes on some things.

Discovering he had a brother had taken him by surprise, but he liked the feeling of having someone around who would depend on him, who wanted to be close to him. He'd never felt the need to bother his mother with his presence, but she'd given him a brother and for that he was grateful.

Dillon took over the chore of helping Wade financially through college. He'd given him advice and concern in addition to loans. After eight years of keeping in touch and visiting whenever possible, they'd developed the kind of blood bond his father had always lectured about. They were brothers, and that counted for a lot.

Dillon stripped off his shirt, then dropped onto the couch, propped his feet on the edge of the battered coffee table and downed his cola in one long gulp.

Wade shook his head. "Look at you! What the hell is wrong with that woman? Why doesn't she want you? I'd give my right ear to have a body like yours."

Dillon choked. "For Christ's sake, Wade, get a grip, will you?" He was well used to Wade's misplaced worship. He'd been putting up with it since the day they'd met, but he still wasn't comfortable with such open adoration.

"It's true," Wade persisted. "All the women at the company want you. The secretaries, the managers, every one of them! As long as I worked there, I never saw anything like it. The female corporate employees are usually so reserved, all buttoned-up businesswomen. Kelsey was the only one who ever paid me any mind. The rest pretty much ignored me. But they *all* gawk at you, and whisper behind their hands. Even Laura Neil, which is nothing short of a miracle."

"Why do you say that?" Dillon was aware of Laura's attention, but it had never felt particularly complimentary. More like wary curiosity.

"Since Cliff took notice of her, she hasn't left his side. She acts like a lapdog."

Dillon scowled at his brother's insulting reference to a lady. "Maybe she's just dedicated."

Wade snorted. "We used to have a thing going, you know. Before I met Kelsey. After we broke up, Cliff promoted Laura to personal assistant. I know he's not really interested. For him, her new position is just a convenience, keeping her close at hand." Wade said it with a sneer, emphasizing his dislike of Cliff Johnson. "Laura hopes he'll marry her, but it'll never happen. Maybe she's realized it, and that's why she's looking at you now. But then, as I said, all the women look at you that way. Kelsey told me some of the women even made bets about who would get you first."

Dillon could only stare. "I don't know about any bets."

"Trust me, the women know." Wade frowned in thought. "It's strange that Virginia is totally immune."

"She's not immune."

"Maybe Virginia's just not...you know." He bobbed his eyebrows suggestively. "Maybe she doesn't prefer men."

Anger surged through him, but he managed to restrain it. The explosive reaction didn't make sense, and he buried it deep, along with all the other confusing emotions he'd experienced tonight, thanks to one Virginia Johnson. "She likes men. There's nothing wrong with Virginia except that she's been given free rein too long. That and too many men wanting her money and not her."

"Not exactly a tough one to figure out." Wade's tone dripped with sarcasm. "Her money is the only appealing thing about her. My position in accounting only put me in direct contact with her a few times, thank God. She scared the hell out of me. With that razor-sharp tongue of hers, she could shred a man to pieces. Besides, she behaves like a dictator."

Actually, Dillon thought, fighting the urge to strangle his brother, Virginia's tongue was soft and tentative and inquisitive. At least when a man took the time to kiss her properly. He had the impression not many men had, and that caused him to feel a certain degree of possessiveness toward her, when he had no right to feel anything at all.

"So what are you going to do now, Dillon?"

"I'm going to wait. She said she'd make a decision this week sometime."

"Kelsey is going to be so disappointed if I don't get this settled soon. She's anxious to move out of the house, to get away from Cliff. She's been biding her time with school and volunteer organizations, but she's miserable."

Dillon shook his head. He'd met Kelsey several times at the company and because of Wade's infatuation he'd paid attention. In Dillon's opinion the woman was a spoiled brat. From what he'd learned of her through subtle queries, both Virginia and Cliff doted on her and tried to protect her from the world. Being the youngest, she'd taken the deaths of her parents the hardest. She was the type of woman Dillon avoided, the type who expected to be coddled and catered to. She knew nothing about coping with real life.

But then, Wade wasn't exactly a model of maturity himself. "You sure this is what you want, Wade? We could still try to fight this in court."

Wade shook his head, frustration apparent in his every feature. "There's no way to get Cliff to drop the embezzlement charges. He's set me up for a reason, and he'll have no qualms about putting me away for good. I don't know what evidence he'll come up with, so there's no way I can fight it, but Kelsey said he's really confident, bragging about nailing me red-handed. So whatever it is, it'll be solid. He'll be sure of that."

Many times, Dillon had considered just beating the hell out of Cliff. It would give him no end of pleasure, yet it wouldn't solve the problem in the long run. Dillon needed to find out what trumped-up evidence Cliff planned to use against Wade. Short of that, he had to find a way to force Cliff to drop the supposed "investigation." If it hadn't been for Kelsey, Wade wouldn't have known of the setup until it was too late. Thankfully, Kelsey had learned of her brother's plan and told Wade.

As yet, no legal charges had been filed, but

Wade had been discharged from his position without pay or benefits while Cliff gathered together his evidence. Once the officials got involved, it would be too late. Time was running out.

Cliff was a powerful man and diffusing this situation wouldn't be easy. Dillon had to pull off a tricky unauthorized private investigation. He had to go through files he had no right to see, search records that weren't his to search and still find a way to keep his own butt out of jail. To do it, he needed Virginia. He didn't want her hurt, but she'd have to be the sacrificial lamb; it couldn't be helped. There was no way to switch course now.

He'd ridden some tricky fences in his day, but this was turning out to be the worst.

Though he already knew the answer, Dillon couldn't stop himself from asking. "Are you sure Cliff wouldn't change his mind if he knew Kelsey was pregnant?"

"Ha! Are you kidding? He'd probably forget handling things 'legally' and just take out a contract on me. He thinks she's way too young to get married."

Dillon hesitated, then leaned forward, propping his elbows on his knees. "You know, Wade, he wouldn't be entirely wrong. Kelsey is only twenty-two, and you're not much older. Marriage isn't something to be rushed into."

Wade stiffened and his hands fisted. "She's pregnant, Dillon. Am I supposed to abandon her now? I know from experience that a woman raising a child alone doesn't have an easy time of it.

The baby deserves a father, and Kelsey deserves a husband."

"There is that, I suppose." Actually, Dillon wished they'd both shown a little more responsibility and not gotten into the situation in the first place, but rehashing that issue wouldn't help now.

Wade began to pace. "It's not like Kelsey is a child. It's just that she's the only family Cliff has. He's very protective of her, and you know my background isn't something to excite a prospective brother-in-law. No man is good enough for Kelsey, but I want a chance to try."

Dillon made a sound of disgust. He hated hearing Wade harp on his unfortunate childhood. So he and their mother hadn't been rich. Dillon and his dad hadn't exactly lived a life of luxury, either. If anything, they'd lived a life of stealth.

None of that came out of his mouth, though. Instead, he heard himself say, "Cliff has Virginia, too."

Wade shook his head in dismissal. "They're not at all close. Virginia is too damn difficult. You know how she always bosses Cliff around. After their parents died, Virginia just took over. He despises her for it."

Dillon suspected that Virginia had taken charge because no one else could. Cliff certainly wouldn't have had the smarts to keep things together. And Kelsey had been a mere teenager. Gritting his teeth, Dillon snarled, "If Virginia means so little to him, then why does he worry so much about who she sees?"

Wade shrugged. "I should think he'd be glad to be rid of her. Most men would be. I suppose Cliff worries about someone marrying Virginia for her money—and her shares in the company. From what I've heard, a few men have tried that tactic, but Cliff doesn't want to take any chances on losing the little control he has."

Dillon surged to his feet. This night wasn't improving with conversation and he needed time alone to put things in perspective. He couldn't allow himself to feel protective of Virginia; he needed the ruthlessness his father had taught him. He needed to be able to do the job, without emotional involvement. "Go home, Wade. I want to get some sleep, and it isn't safe for you to hang around here for long. If anyone finds out we're related, the whole plan is ruined."

"I know. And I'm sorry. But I just couldn't wait."

"You're going to have to wait from now on." He spoke sternly in the way he knew commanded attention. "Don't come here again. Do you understand?" He waited until Wade nodded, then he added, "I'll get in touch with you when I find out something."

Reluctantly, Wade turned away. "All right." He walked to the door and then paused. "You know how much I appreciate all this, don't you, Dillon? I didn't have anyone else to turn to. The one lawyer I spoke with was useless. He said the company probably wouldn't press charges because they'd most likely want to avoid the scandal and the possibility of being discredited in front of their shareholders. If it was anyone but

Cliff, I'd agree. But he won't be happy just firing me. He wants to ruin me completely. Kelsey and I didn't know what to do. Against Cliff's money, I didn't stand a chance. He'll be sure to have the best lawyers around and they'll make mincemeat out of me. I'd already be in jail and Kelsey would have to raise our baby alone. Cliff would have given her a hard time over the scandal—"

"Enough already, Wade." Damn, but the rambling melodramatics were enough to make him sick. Wade had missed his calling. Instead of becoming an accountant, he should have joined the theater. Still, Wade was his brother, so Dillon forgave him his shortcomings, just as he hoped to be forgiven for his own. "I told you I'd take care of things and I will."

Wade nodded once more, sent his brother a shaky, endearingly familial smile, then left.

Dillon locked up the apartment and turned out the lights.

When he was finally alone with his thoughts, he wondered if he was doing the right thing. Maybe he should have tried to raise enough money to get good legal representation for Wade. Not the low-rate lawyer Wade had spoken with, but a sharpshooter who could match Cliff's. Dillon had property in Mexico he could have sold. That would have meant starting over, but then, he'd started over many times. He liked his home, but there were higher priorities to consider; he had to think about his father, too.

His dad lived with him now, and Dillon didn't want to uproot him. His father wasn't a young man anymore, and he had a few health problems thanks to the hard life he'd led.

Besides, if Virginia had been a typical female, this whole thing would have been simple. But no, she had to be difficult and unique and a pain in the backside. He'd never known a woman like her.

Naked, he slid between the sheets and stacked his hands behind his head. It was dark and cold and snowflakes patterned his window, making the moonlight look like lace against the far wall. He wondered how Virginia would react when she realized his sole interest in her was her personal files. He wondered how she'd react to the news that her twenty-two-year-old pampered baby sister was pregnant and wanted to marry Wade, a man accused of embezzlement, a man with a less than sterling background. *A man related to him.*

Most of all, he wondered how Virginia would react when she found out he wasn't the wimp she assumed him to be. Would she cry with hurt? He closed his eyes at the vision and shuddered with reaction.

Whatever she did, it wouldn't be the expected. There wasn't another woman like her anywhere, and she had the knack of keeping him on his toes. She wouldn't make his job easy.

But he'd bet his last breath she'd make it interesting.

3

DILLON WAS IN Cliff's office when Virginia rushed in two days later. Lounged back on his spine in a casual sprawl, his legs wide, he made her forget why she'd wanted to see Cliff in the first place. Virginia noticed how the soft, worn material of his dark jeans cupped his heavy sex. His hands rested over a taut flat belly and his shoulders stretched the pressed material of his dress shirt. His hair hung to his shoulders, his collar was unbuttoned and his sleeves were rolled up. Her gaze traveled over him until she met his eyes. She shivered.

He looked totally relaxed, but his brown eyes were alert. She loved it when he acted so defiantly arrogant for her brother's sake. It made him look sexy and sinful and her heart immediately picked up rhythm.

She forced her gaze to where her brother sat behind a massive desk. One concern was replaced with another.

"What's he doing here, Cliff? Has there been some kind of trouble?" In the normal course of his job, Dillon didn't have much call to hang around Cliff's office.

Cliff glared at her—a look to which she was

well accustomed to. "He's my head of security. Why shouldn't he be here?"

She strolled across the floor, trying not to react to the almost tactile sensation of Dillon's eyes on her as he tracked her every step. Propping her hip on the edge of Cliff's desk, she asked, "Are we considering making some kind of adjustment or improvement? Is that why he's here?"

Cliff slammed down the pen he'd been doodling with. "Damn it, Virginia, don't you have a diet class or something to go to?"

That hurt. Her weight had always been a problem, but it wasn't something she wanted to discuss in front of Dillon. Usually the clothes she wore were loose enough so as not to accent the more obvious trouble spots. Today, her simple wool tunic over matching slacks worked wonders—or so she'd thought. Now she was uncomfortably aware of the width of her hips, the weight of her breasts, the roundness of her belly and thighs. She wanted to escape both men's scrutiny.

She lifted her chin. Low blows were a specialty of Cliff's. She should have become immune to them by now.

She didn't dare glance at Dillon. She didn't want to know what he thought of her brother's comment or, at the moment, what he thought of her. "I'm a busy woman, Brother, but I think I can spare some time to see what you're screwing up now."

Cliff snarled, almost ready to explode. At the last second he pulled himself together and sent Dillon an exasperated look of shared male insight, as if to say, *Women.* Virginia stiffened. Fighting Cliff had become a way of life, both in business and in her personal pride. "You do remember, don't you, Cliff, that any decisions have to go through me first?"

"How could I forget with you forever shoving it in my face?"

"So?" She waited, and finally he turned a sheath of papers toward her.

She studied the new property sheets for a moment before commenting. "The Eastland project." She ignored Cliff's surprise. He should know by now that there was no facet of the business she wasn't fully aware of. The company was her life, the only thing she was truly good at. She wouldn't let anything slip by her.

She approved the idea of expansion by purchasing the retail property in Eastland. Once the new expressway was built, the mall would flourish. Time and invested money were all they needed, and Johnson's Sporting Goods had both. Their expansion would add new life to the floundering area, drawing in other retailers.

"Actually, it looks good. Send some copies to my office today and I'll let you know later exactly what I think."

Through gritted teeth, Cliff told her, "Everything has been worked out. The security upgrades have even been tested and approved. I planned to work out a deal today."

"No. Not until I've had more time to study the cost sheets. There's no rush. It takes time to—"

Cliff shoved back his chair and stood. Startled,

Virginia glanced up. He was practically seething, his hands curled into fists at his sides.

"There'll come a point, Virginia, when you push me too far!" He turned to Dillon and barked, "Be upstairs in the conference room in ten minutes."

He stormed out and Virginia was left there with her mouth hanging open and an uncomfortable silence disturbing the air. It wasn't like Cliff to put on such a display in front of employees.

Without really wanting to, she looked over at Dillon. He hadn't moved. He seemed unperturbed by Cliff's overreaction, but his dark eyes were cryptic. She tried a shaky smile. For some stupid reason she felt defensive. Having the world know her own brother reviled her had the same effect as being nicknamed "Chubby" in grade school.

"Well, I certainly pushed the wrong buttons this morning, didn't I?" she said, relying on flippancy to save her pride.

Dillon narrowed his eyes. "Or the right ones."

"What does that mean?"

"Why do you deliberately provoke him, Virginia?"

She pushed away from the desk and started for the door. Discussing family business with employees—regardless of how gorgeous they might be—wasn't done. Still, she couldn't resist one righteous parting shot. "I have as much right to know what's going on in this company as he does. Or more so!" When she turned, Dillon was right behind her. She gasped, took a step back and hit the door. She hadn't even heard him move.

He took another step closer, looming over her. His fingers touched her chin; his dark gaze touched everywhere else. In a rumble, he whispered, "There are gentler ways for a woman to get what she wants. Especially from her own brother."

For one instant she felt frozen by his touch. Her stomach curled and her nipples tightened into sensitive peaks. Then she shook her head. "So I should play meek and mild just to placate Cliff? I don't have a meek or mild bone in my body. I thought you understood that, Dillon."

He didn't smile. "Are you going to make time for me this weekend, Virginia?"

"Are you being pushy?" she asked automatically, still stinging from her brother's remarks.

To her disappointment, he backed down, both physically and mentally. For a single heartbeat, he looked frustrated, almost angry, but he took a safe step away from her and shook his head. "No, of course not. I'm just...anxious."

If he was really anxious, he'd insist she make a decision, she thought. But then, it wasn't fair of her to try to force her own dominant spirit on him. She went on tiptoe to kiss his chin. "I need to be here Friday for a meeting, but I can take off Thursday."

His gaze heated. "What time?"

"Whenever you like. You tell me."

Without hesitation, he said, "Early. We could spend the entire day together. The waiting is just about killing me."

After her brother's crack about her weight, Dillon's obvious desire was a welcome balm. She pressed closer to him for a kiss and felt his large hand cup her backside, gently squeezing. With her brother's comment still lingering fresh in her mind, she was uncomfortable with the touch and stepped away. His gaze searched her face, questioning, and she tried not to blush.

Other men who had come on to her had been discreet with their touches, never venturing so boldly in broad daylight as Dillon seemed prepared to do. In thirty years, she'd had two lovers, and they'd both made it a practice to have sex in the dark and under the covers, which suited her just fine. The entire experience had always been rather nice. Safe and predictable and uncomplicated. The sex itself hadn't been spectacular, but the sharing, the holding and touching had comforted her in a way nothing else could.

She hoped Dillon wouldn't prove too difficult about the arrangement. Surely he'd be satisfied with proper bedroom convention.

"This isn't exactly the best place, is it, Dillon?"

At first he didn't answer and her heart raced in both dread and anticipation. He shook his head. "No, it isn't. I'm sorry."

Virginia sighed. "Since I know you're worried about appearances, we'll meet in the mall parking lot by my home. That way no one will see us leaving."

"Can you be ready at six?"

"*That* early?"

His tone dropped to a husky rumble. "It'll give us more time together."

"All right, then." She smiled. "Where did you want to go?"

Dillon hesitated, then touched her cheek again. "Why don't you let me take care of that. It'll be a surprise."

"Hmm. A secret?"

He nodded. "What did you need to see Cliff about?"

She stared into his eyes, amazed by the mixed messages there. Hunger, but also…regret?

"Virginia?"

"What?"

He laughed, a low, rough sound that made her belly tingle. "You rushed in here to see Cliff, but got sidetracked. Was it important?"

"Oh." She paused. "Oh! Damn it, I needed to talk to him. Something's wrong with my car. I wanted to use his."

"That's not a problem." He dug in his pocket and pulled out a large key ring, then unhooked one gold key. "Here. You can use the company car. I left it in the garage, lower level, personnel entrance. But what's wrong with yours? Maybe I can help you with it."

"I'm not sure." Virginia accepted the key, feeling awkward with Dillon's concern. She wasn't used to anyone asking after her in such a solicitous way. For as long as she could remember, she'd taken care of herself. "Something's wrong with the brakes. I started out of the parking lot, then remembered some papers I needed on my desk. When I went to put on the brakes, they felt sluggish at first, not really catching, and when I pumped them, the pedal went all the way to the

floor. I ran into a guardrail." She scowled, thinking of the damage that had been done to her
bumper. "It's lucky I found out they weren't
working before I tried to leave the garage. You
know how the exit ramp slopes down right into
the main road."

"And into heavy traffic," he added in an omi-
nous whisper. Dillon's brows were lowered and
a muscle ticked in his jaw. Suddenly, his arms
surrounded her and he gave her a tight squeeze.
With his mouth against her neck, he murmured,
"You could have been killed."

Pushing herself away from his hard chest, Virginia laughed, trying to make light of his reaction. "Nonsense! It wasn't all that dramatic or life
threatening, I promise. I'd barely gone three feet
before I found out they weren't working. But I do
intend to give my serviceman a piece of my
mind. I had my oil changed not two weeks ago
and he told me he'd topped off all the fluids."

Dillon bent to press his forehead to hers. "I'll
take a look at it. You…might have had some
damage to the brake lines."

Virginia shook her head. "Dillon, looking after
my car isn't part of your job and not at all a necessary part of our relationship. Besides, I already
called the tow truck. I can take care of myself,
you know."

He looked as if he wanted to argue, but held
his tongue. In this instance, Virginia appreciated
his restraint. She liked her independence and
wanted no infringements on it. She smiled her
approval. "You know, it's too bad I have to check
in here Friday morning." She smoothed her open

palm over his wide chest and sighed. "I think I'd like a lot more time with you, truth be told."

His slight frown and the darkening of his eyes were confusing. He reached around her and opened the door, suddenly in a hurry to leave. On his way out, he muttered gruffly, "Save your wishes for something important, honey. You never know when you might need them."

She wondered what he meant, or if he'd meant anything at all. Dillon was an elusive man and most times she wasn't at all sure how to take him. But she did feel certain about one thing. She would definitely enjoy her fling with him.

"DON'T EVER SPEAK to me like a lackey again."

Cliff whirled around and stared. Dillon closed the door quietly behind him and stalked forward. He knew he wasn't precisely angry at Cliff, at least not over anything new. But he made a fine target. And right now, Dillon needed an outlet.

He hadn't reached Virginia's car before it was taken away, but he'd still had his suspicions confirmed. Someone had cut her brake lines. Reddish brake fluid made a large puddle where her car had been parked. This was no mere leak.

Cliff backed up two steps before he caught himself. "What are you talking about?"

Dillon flattened his palms on the highly polished table and leaned toward Cliff. "Don't give me orders. If you want to meet with me, say so, but don't get pissed off at your sister and then bark at me."

Cliff tried a show of umbrage. "Now, see here…"

"I'm a damn good employee, Cliff. I've upgraded your entire security system and saved you a bundle in the process. I've found glitches most men would never have noticed. That's my job and I do it well. But I don't need this job and I don't need to be talked down to. Understand?"

Dillon was pushing it, but Cliff seemed to gain more respect for him every time he asserted himself. Unlike Virginia. It made sense to Dillon. He'd be damned if he'd want some marshmallow in charge of protecting the interests of his company. Not only was Dillon in charge of securing the actual property against theft, both at the offices where Cliff and Virginia worked and at the retail outlets, but he evaluated the security potential and estimated costs of future retail sites. He also oversaw the personal security for employees, including the boss. Johnson's Sporting Goods wasn't a nickle and dime operation.

Dillon recognized his value to the Johnsons. He'd learned his trade from the best. His father had taught him how to secure, and how to breach, the legal and the illegal, which made him unique, and one of the best in the business.

Cliff needed him, especially with Virginia constantly breathing down his neck.

Besides, now that he believed Virginia was being threatened, he wasn't quite up to maintaining his pretense with Cliff. Virginia had finally agreed to some intimate time alone with him, and it was entirely possible he'd be able to settle things just by getting a few good leads from her.

Surely Virginia would know what trumped up evidence Cliff had manufactured. If she would talk.

God, he hoped it would work out that simply. He hated playing the dutiful employee. He preferred working for himself, hiring himself out on short-term jobs, spending his free time in Mexico with his father and his horses and his land.

Dillon figured that once he established a relationship with Virginia, he could quit the company. Virginia would undoubtedly find him more appealing as a free agent; there would be no reason for her to think she was being used.

Dillon shook his head. He didn't like the warmth that swelled over him when he considered pleasing her. It didn't matter what Virginia thought or would think. If her bright golden eyes were angry or aroused. None of it mattered. None of it *could* matter.

A heartfelt sigh from Cliff broke into Dillon's thoughts.

"You're right," Cliff said. "I do value you as an employee. It's just that Virginia can be so damn arrogant, and I've got enough on my mind right now without her harassment."

Very slowly, Dillon straightened. "Oh? Anything I can help with?" Little by little, Cliff opened up to him, making him a confidant, wanting him for a cohort in his grievances against his sister.

Cliff waved dismissively. "It's a matter that came up before you were hired. I have people already on the problem."

"What exactly is the problem?"

"A little matter of internal embezzlement. A former employee used his position to siphon funds from the company. The theft occurred mostly in insubstantial amounts, so it was hard to notice. I knew it was him, and I fired him on the spot, but of course I can't accuse him officially without solid evidence. Finding proof is taking some doing. You know how difficult it can be to trace numbers. However, I believe we finally have him nailed. We should be able to wrap things up any day now."

"What kind of evidence do you have?" Keeping his tone so mild, so bland, was more than difficult when he wanted to grab Cliff and slam his fist in his mouth. He wanted to force him to admit it was all a scam. Wade couldn't be guilty.

Except...Cliff didn't look as though he was scamming. He looked smugly confident. It shook Dillon.

"My lawyers have advised me not to discuss the case. Suffice it to say, when we go to court, we won't lose." He pushed a button on the intercom, then requested that Laura bring in coffee. Cliff stacked some files and turned to face Dillon. "The others will be joining me soon, but I wanted to talk with you for a minute or two first. Virginia interrupted us downstairs. But now is as good a time as any."

This was curious. Dillon considered telling Cliff why Virginia had interrupted, about the cut brake lines, but decided against it. Cliff could be the very one who had tampered with Virginia's car. At the moment, he wasn't willing to put family loyalty to the test, especially not in Cliff's case.

Dillon hid his thoughts well as he gave Cliff his attention. "I didn't realize we were having a meeting. Is your sister invited to this one?"

"Hell no." Cliff chuckled. "I try to keep her as much out of the way as possible. You've seen firsthand how offensive she can be. No, the meeting is about expanding the downtown operation."

Not again, Dillon thought, tired of that tune and trying to explain to an idiot that opening an outlet downtown was a waste of funds. Unless the entire area was revamped, Cliff would be better off withdrawing and investing his money on renovations elsewhere. Though Virginia had told Cliff that countless times, it didn't take someone with her business sense to see it. Dillon had backed up her reasoning, on a security level. Cliff wasn't listening.

"You know how I feel about that, Cliff. I can upgrade all the systems there, hire good people to work in shifts, but it won't do you any good. Even without the petty theft, which is rampant and you know it, that store is a money hog. There's not enough business to warrant the effort."

Cliff gestured with his hand, looking distracted and annoyed. "That's not what I want to speak to you about. No, I want to talk to you about my sister."

Dillon turned his back to look out the third-story windows. Below him was human congestion, smog and noise. The sides of the street were piled high with blackened snow and sludge. Traffic flowed, the same traffic Virginia had almost encountered, without brakes. He shuddered.

He hated being here in Delaport City on this ridiculous ruse. He wanted to be home again, listening to his father grumbling and recounting all his old adventures. This didn't feel like an adventure. This felt like one huge mistake. "You want to talk about your sister? What about her?"

"I, ah, know from your file that your expertise includes surveillance."

"My *expertise* covers a lot of activities that aren't exactly part of a legitimate job résumé, especially not for the position you hired me for. I only gave you a few facts because I figured you'd need something to recommend me." The information was accurate, just in case Cliff had the sense to look, which Dillon wasn't certain of. But Virginia would have checked, of that he had no doubt. So he'd supplied the names of the few companies he'd ever worked for. Like his father, he could ferret out trouble—or cause it. With equal success, according to who was paying the most. It wasn't a trait he felt any particular pride over. Just a way of survival.

"Virginia insisted on checking into your employment background. She was impressed, which says a lot, even though your lack of consistency with any one job concerned her. Has she ever spoken to you about it?"

Dillon still faced the window. He was afraid if he looked at Cliff, all his anger would show. "No. Other than a few casual exchanges, we've never spoken."

"Excellent! Then she'll never suspect you."

"Suspect me of what?" He did turn to Cliff now. "What is it you want me to do?"

"I want you to spy on her, of course. She's up to something, seeing someone. God only knows what that woman's capable of."

Dillon grunted. He knew she was capable of making grown men cower, of scaring off any advances, of isolating herself completely with her sharp tongue and smothering arrogance. She was also capable of making him burn red-hot.

Was she capable of making an enemy who would wish her harm?

Dillon shook his head, feeling his tension simmer once again. "What do you mean, she's seeing someone?"

"The other night at the party, I caught her sneaking back into the kitchen."

With a dry look, Dillon said, "I can't imagine Virginia *sneaking* anywhere. It's not in her nature."

"No, you're right. She strutted back into the house, bold as you please, when she'd been out there conspiring with someone against me."

Dillon pulled out a chair and straddled it. Cliff's stupidity never ceased to amaze him. "Conspiring? How do you know she wasn't with a lover?"

He grinned. "That's exactly what she said! How about that—you two share a similar sense of humor."

Dillon heard a noise and looked up. Laura Neil stood in the doorway, holding a tray with fresh coffee and two mugs. Dillon wondered how long she'd been standing there, but then decided it didn't matter. He was more interested in the way the woman watched Cliff, sheer adoration clouding her eyes.

Cliff nodded to her and she entered. She leaned close to him while she poured the coffee, and asked if they needed anything else. Every so often, her gaze darted to Dillon. He almost felt sorry for her. It was obvious she was infatuated with Cliff, and just as obvious that Cliff had used his position to take advantage of her. To Dillon's mind, it was one more reason to despise Virginia's brother.

Cliff dismissed Laura. Dillon sipped from his cup, waiting. He knew his silence would annoy Cliff, so therefore his patience was its own reward.

After only a few seconds, Cliff exploded. "Well? What do you say?"

Dillon glanced at him over his mug. "To what? You haven't asked me anything yet."

"Oh, for... Will you check into it? Find out what Virginia is up to and who she's involved with?"

"What's in it for me?"

"A five-hundred-dollar bonus. Twice that if you come up with something concrete."

The irony of it amused Dillon—that Cliff would be paying Dillon to spy on himself. But the little bastard was also spying on his sister, and Dillon's suspicions were growing. He didn't trust Cliff, not at all.

Dillon let Cliff wait while he pretended to think things over. Of course he'd agree to do it. It made perfect sense. If *he* was checking into things, Cliff wouldn't be hiring someone else who would get in his way.

Dragging out the inevitable, and hoping for any tidbit of information that might help him, Dillon asked, "Any clues at all who it might be? Any leads?"

"Just the obvious. The guy must be someone who could benefit Virginia in some way, someone in the company who might be able to sway votes."

From what he'd heard, Virginia always won every vote, so that theory didn't make sense. He refrained from pointing that out to Cliff. "Anything else?"

Cliff shrugged. "The guy's most likely passive, ineffectual, a spineless sort. You know how Virginia is. She'd never be able to get a man like you to put up with her carping and demands for some scheme of hers. And Virginia insists on complete obedience. She wouldn't accept any defiance."

Dillon couldn't help himself; he grinned. "So I'm looking for a wimp?" The description was apt.

"Yes, but a wimp with connections. Someone who could do her some good."

"But you're a hundred percent positive she's not involved in a personal relationship she just doesn't want you to know about?"

Cliff was already shaking his head. "Not Virginia. Men are interested in her for one reason—to use her. And I'd want to know about that, too. Even though she's sworn she'll never marry, I have to protect her from those sorts. She's too abrasive and too overweight to attract anyone with genuine feelings. She'd only end up hurt, or hurting the company."

Abruptly, Dillon came to his feet. One more second with the loving brother and he'd throw him out the damn window. "I'll check into things." He crossed to the door, then turned back. "By the way, Virginia had some brake trouble today." He watched Cliff closely, waiting.

"Oh?"

"She's all right, but her car's out of commission for a while. I gave her the company car to use."

Cliff waved a hand, already distracted, as he gathered together the notes for his meeting. "That's fine."

Dillon clenched his jaw. He hadn't been asking for permission, but rather watching for a reaction. He didn't get one.

He jerked the door open and started out, saying over his shoulder, "I'm taking the rest of the day off. I'll be in touch later."

Cliff didn't argue. He couldn't have anyway. Dillon had already slammed the door.

4

Virginia had just hung up the phone when the rap sounded on her office door. She glanced up, frustrated by the way her day had gone. First the problems with her car, then her run-in with Cliff. And her meeting hadn't gone at all well. Today was not her day, and she was tired. A hot bath and a long night's sleep seemed just the cure.

"Come in."

Dillon stuck his head in the door. "You about ready to head home?"

As always, one glance into those sinfully dark eyes turned her insides warm and jittery. With every minute that passed, she anticipated her day alone with him more. "Mmm. I was just about to call a cab. What's up?"

She didn't particularly relish the idea of doing any more business tonight, but for Dillon, she'd make an exception. Spending time with him was seldom a hardship.

He stepped into her office and closed the door behind him. His features were etched in a frown. Virginia sighed, knowing why he'd come by. "If you're here to tell me about Cliff's plans to rework the downtown office, I've heard all about it."

Dillon stiffened. "It's not my job to tattle on your damn brother."

She lifted a brow at his tone as well as his words. "No? Your loyalty to a prospective lover doesn't go quite that far?" Virginia knew she was taunting him, but damn it, her day had been rotten, and just once, she wanted to see Dillon lose his temper, cut loose and prove to her what a powerful man he could be. But instead, he merely narrowed his eyes and waited.

Virginia took pity on him. "I'm sorry. I was just about to head home and I'm a little out of sorts. It hasn't been the best of days."

"That's why I'm here," he said. "To offer you a ride."

"Chauffeuring is part of your job description?"

"Why not?" He stepped closer, his expression inscrutable. "I'm in charge of security. It's my responsibility to see that you make it home safely."

She couldn't help but smile. "That's stretching it, Dillon."

"Not so." He looked at her intently, his gaze unwavering. "I think your brake lines might have been tampered with."

She waited for the punch line, and when it didn't come she got to her feet and crossed to the closet to retrieve her coat. Before she could slip it on, Dillon was behind her, holding her shoulders. "I'm serious, Virginia."

"That's ridiculous." She turned to face him. "So some vandal picked our parking lot to play around in. We'll just increase security."

"That's just it." He raised his hand to her

cheek and stroked it. "Maybe it wasn't a vandal. Maybe whoever did it targeted your car."

"So now I have an enemy?" She could see he was serious, but she couldn't feel the same way. It was entirely too far-fetched. "You've been working too hard, Dillon. I think you need a day off more than I do."

His jaw tightened and his hands slipped to her shoulders again. After a deep calming breath, he said, "All right, then just humor me, okay? Let me drive you home tonight."

"I'm a big girl, Dillon, all grown-up. I don't need a caretaker."

He smiled, a beautiful smile that made her toes curl. He kissed her and she forgot they were standing in the middle of her office and someone could walk in at any moment.

He pulled back only far enough to speak, but his breath was warm on her lips, his tone husky. "You don't have to convince me of that, honey. I know it all too well." He kissed her again, a quick, hard kiss, then stepped back. "What did your mechanic say?"

Virginia had trouble bringing herself back under control. Lord love him, the man was a temptation, and she was quickly growing tired of resisting him. She stared up at him and tried to find her aplomb.

"I haven't talked with my mechanic yet. He won't have a chance to look at the car until tomorrow."

"Then will you please—for my sake—be extra cautious until then?"

She thought about denying him, if for no other

reason than reasserting her independence. She'd always had to fight so hard to prove herself, she sometimes didn't know when to quit fighting. But truth be told, she loved the idea of him taking her home. Maybe he'd come inside, maybe he'd stop being so skittish about appearances and make love to her this very night. The mere thought caused her body to heat. "All right."

Dillon stared down at her a moment longer before he nodded. He held her coat while she slipped into it, then led her out the door.

DILLON DIDN'T WANT to explore his satisfaction too deeply. Having Virginia accede to his wishes made him feel like a conqueror. It hadn't happened often, and he had a feeling it wouldn't happen again any time soon. Virginia wasn't a woman to let a man call the shots. Right now, she was quiet. Too quiet. And he wondered if maybe she was regretting her small show of weakness. He didn't consider caution a weakness, but he knew she would.

"Turn left up here."

Startled out of his thoughts, Dillon reminded himself that he wasn't supposed to know where she lived. He had to keep his mind on what he was doing, rather than trying to dissect Virginia's psyche. He'd already discovered many times over what a futile and frustrating effort that could be. He just couldn't seem to help himself; she fascinated him.

For the rest of the ride, he waited for her directions, even though he knew the way. Before getting hired on at Johnson's Sporting Goods, he'd done a complete check on her.

When they pulled into her driveway, Virginia started to open her door. Dillon ignored that and walked around to her side of the car. She stood there, embraced by selective moonlight, on this dark, cloudy night. Her head was tilted back as she stared up at him, her eyes wide, and he wanted her.

He hated himself for it, but he wanted her. The iron control he'd always depended on seemed to evaporate where this woman was concerned, and it didn't make sense. He didn't even like her.

"Do you want to come in for a while?"

He hesitated. It didn't take a genius to see the direction of her thoughts and, seeing that, he become instantly, painfully, hard. But making love to Virginia, especially now, wasn't a wise thing to contemplate. He racked his brain for any excuse that would be believable, but before he could speak, a shadow caught his eye and he jerked toward the house. He could have sworn he saw a curtain move.

He shoved Virginia behind him as he stepped deeper into the shadows. "Do you have any pets, honey?"

"No. Dillon what are you—"

"Shh. Someone's in your house." His senses rioted, telling him all he needed to know.

"What?"

"Give me your key."

Thankfully, Virginia complied, but when he told her to get into his car and lock the doors, she refused. As he inched closer to the house, she followed, leaving him no choice but to stop. "Damn it, Virginia." His whispered voice was guttural, his temper on the edge. He grasped her shoulders. "You can't—"

"It's my house. I know my way around a lot better than you do."

He shook her. He hadn't meant to, but she was so obstinate, so annoying, he couldn't help himself. "This isn't a game, damn it! For once, will you—"

They both heard the back door slam, the sound carried easily on the cold, quiet night. Dillon squeezed her shoulders hard. "Stay put!"

He took off at a run. Even before he reached the backyard, he knew the chase was useless. Woods bordered her property on two sides, and he had no doubt the intruder would have long vanished into the black shadows. He cursed, then cursed again when Virginia touched his arm and he almost threw her to the ground in reaction. In the split second before he touched her, he realized who she was.

Without a word, knowing she wouldn't follow an order even if her life depended on it, he dragged her up the back steps and into the house, keeping to the side so he wouldn't destroy any footprints that might have been left behind. His temper was on the ragged edge, the ruthless aspects of his personality ruling him.

He found two light switches just inside the door. One illuminated the kitchen with blinding fluorescent light and the other flooded the backyard. Dillon scanned the yard, but there wasn't a single movement caught in the glare.

"Call the police," he whispered.

She answered in kind. "Why? Whoever it was is long gone now."

"Unless there was more than one guy. Just do it."

She bristled, but he didn't have time to cajole her. He waited only until he saw her lift the receiver, then cautiously made his way down the hall, turning on lights as he went. Quickly, methodically, he went through the downstairs rooms, then trotted silently up the carpeted stairway to the upper level. He had explored all the rooms before Virginia finished making the call.

"Dillon?"

"It's okay." He answered from her bedroom, the last room he'd found. Virginia joined him there.

She glanced around, looking uncomfortable. "The police are on their way. They said to stay in the kitchen, not to try to be a hero."

He grunted. "This is what I'm trained to do, Virginia."

"To be a hero?"

He knew she was teasing. He could see it her golden eyes, shining now from the excitement. He shook his head. "Your bedroom is a surprise."

That small observation removed the smile from her lips. She stiffened and drew her auburn brows together. "What's that supposed to mean?"

He left the room, Virginia hot on his heels. With a deliberate shrug, he said, "It's a little more feminine than I had expected, that's all. I mean, I hadn't pictured you having ruffled pillow shams or lace curtains."

She apparently didn't know what to say to that, so Dillon changed the subject. "How about some coffee?" He approached the back door, examining it closely. "I'm sure the cops would appreciate it on a cold night like this."

He'd no sooner said the words than the sirens could be heard. Sure enough, the police were more than willing to swill coffee as they gave the house another examination. To everyone's surprise except maybe Dillon's, nothing seemed to be missing.

Still, the police wrote up the incident as a simple break and enter.

One young officer held his hat in one hand while cradling his coffee in the other. "With a house like yours, in this neighborhood, a burglar would be in heaven."

Another policeman confirmed what Dillon already knew. "They came in through the kitchen door."

"But how?" Virginia didn't seem unsettled by the whole affair—she seemed furious. "My doors are always locked."

"They picked the lock somehow." The cop shrugged. "Leave your floodlights on tonight. In fact, you should get a timer to turn them on as soon as it gets dark. And put in an alarm system, as well. A woman living here alone—"

Disgusted, Dillon interrupted. "I'll see to it tomorrow."

Virginia frowned at him, but kept her peace. Dillon's position, his reason for being with her, had already been explained. Since then the cops had been giving him a wide berth.

The policeman nodded. "Yeah, well, we'll patrol through the neighborhood the rest of the night, ma'am. You should be safe enough. Very seldom does a perpetrator return once he knows he's been discovered."

Dillon didn't agree, and he told Virginia so as soon as the officers had left. "You shouldn't stay here."

"Now, don't start, Dillon. I'm tired and I want to go to bed. I'm not about to start uprooting myself tonight."

He paced, trying to think while she glared at him, looking her most imperious. "What is the matter with you? You've been entirely too high-handed this evening and I've about had enough!"

He should have known she'd get her back up and make this more difficult than it had to be. "Virginia, has it escaped your notice that you've been threatened twice in the same day?"

She rolled her eyes. "I've had car trouble and a simple break-in. That's doesn't exactly add up to a life-or-death situation."

He clenched his fists tight, fighting for control. It seemed he fought that particular battle more since meeting Virginia than he ever had in his entire life. "How do you think the guy got inside?"

She shrugged. "He picked the lock."

"There's no evidence of a forced entry. What if he had a key?"

Her eyes widened and she took a step back.

"What exactly are you saying, Dillon? You think someone I know is trying to hurt me? Who?"

He should probably have admitted his suspicions that he thought Cliff might very well be the one harassing her. But something held him back. Despite all her bravado, all her indignation and affronted pride, she was still a woman, soft and vulnerable. From what he knew of her, Virginia had never had an easy life, and she'd never had anyone to love her. To find out now just how big a scoundrel her brother could be might well devastate her. He couldn't bear that.

To his shame, though, he had another reason for hesitating. The possibility that if he forced the issue, she might blame Wade for threatening her. To Virginia, Wade would be a much more likely suspect. Her brother had accused him of embezzlement, and he'd been fired. Didn't that give Wade motive enough, in her mind, to want revenge? If he convinced her the threats were real, would it backfire on Wade?

Wade could end up being accused not only as an embezzler, but an assailant as well. And then, if Virginia thought Wade was guilty, she would let her guard down. The real assailant would have a clear field. It was too risky. And if Virginia got hurt because he was preoccupied with his brother…

Impulsively, he put his arms around her and pulled her close in a careful hug. She resisted, holding herself stiff in his arms until he said, "I'm sorry. I know I've been on edge tonight. But Virginia, at least give me the right to worry about you a little, okay?"

She smiled up at him. "If you insist. But it isn't necessary. I'll be careful. I'm not an idiot."

"I know." He kissed her and didn't want to stop kissing her. Her lips were warm and soft and she tempted him. He opened his mouth over hers, gently moving, savoring her taste. She made a small sound deep in her throat when his tongue licked over her bottom lip.

Cursing inwardly, Dillon set her away from him and reached for his coat. "Will you be all right tonight?"

He could tell by her expression that she wanted to ask him to stay; pride would keep her from it, though. And this time, he was glad. In less than twenty-four hours, everything had changed. His plans thrown into turmoil, he had to adapt. False accusations of embezzlement were no longer the only issue, and took a back seat to Virginia's safety. This new threat was much more tangible, much more immediate.

He felt responsible for Virginia, whether she liked it or not, and he'd do his best to protect her, even while helping his brother. If he had to be ruthless to accomplish both goals, so be it. In all fairness, he gave her one last chance to do things the easy way. "Why don't you take a vacation? Disappear for a while until things calm down?"

"What things? You really are overreacting."

His hands fisted at his sides. "This wasn't a simple break-in, Virginia."

"Of course it was—"

"Nothing was taken, damn it! How do you explain that?"

She shrugged. "It's like the police said. We probably interrupted the burglar."

He grabbed her arms, his patience at an end. "What if you'd walked in here alone? What if I hadn't been with you? Do you think whoever it was would have run?"

She stared at him blankly, her lips parted in surprise at his vehemence. With an effort, he eased his tone.

"This is what I do, honey. I know what I'm talking about. To be safe, you should get out of here for a while. Go to a motel. I'll join you Thursday, just as we planned."

She rubbed his shoulder as if to soothe him. "I have responsibilities here, Dillon. And the police really don't seem to think there's anything to be alarmed about."

Dillon drew a deep breath and released her. "Surely the company can survive without you for a few days." Without having to worry about her being threatened and with free run of her office, he could not only get the information he needed to absolve Wade, but most likely nail the bastard who was harassing her as well. All he needed was a little time.

She began loading empty coffee cups into the dishwasher, and when she glanced at him, a gentleness had entered her eyes. "I like you, Dillon, and I want to spend time with you. But one long afternoon will have to be enough for now. Don't ask for more. My first priority will always be running the company—you know that."

Only, it wasn't her company, it was Cliff's.

And Dillon had a feeling Cliff had gotten tired of sharing it with her.

Her stubbornness knew no bounds; she wouldn't relent. He closed his eyes a moment, accepting the inevitable, knowing what had to be done, knowing his options had just become severely limited. From the moment he'd involved himself in this mess, he'd felt equal parts protective and possessive of her. He wouldn't let anyone hurt her. He'd protect her despite herself. Never mind that she'd probably despise him for it. Her hate had been guaranteed from the first.

He had one more day, Wednesday, to watch over her, while at the same time rearranging his plans and making new ones. He had a lot to accomplish in the time left to him, including the installation of an alarm system at her house that would put a stop to intruders.

He sighed as the ramifications of his new plan sank in. Virginia would miss her meeting on Friday after all. But at least she'd be safe.

And Dillon understood why. Cliff had given Shelai that up a couple two...

Her smile wavered. After a few moments, she wouldn't quote. He...d and...begin a moment accepting the inevitable, know me, what had to be done. Show me not against that just...because se wanted him not from the moment he'd involved

5

DILLON HEARD the ringing as if from far away. It pierced his subconsciousness, but wasn't enough to get him out of the dream. And he knew he was dreaming, knew it wasn't real, but he couldn't force himself awake.

The cell was dark and cold, and in his dream he accepted that he would spend many years there, yet strangely enough, that wasn't what bothered him most. No, it was Virginia, standing outside his cell, round with a late pregnancy. His child. He broke out in a sweat. Cliff was pointing and laughing from the background, and Virginia's eyes looked wounded—and accusing.

The ringing became more insistent, sounding like a small scream, and he jerked awake. His heart thundered and all his muscles felt too tight, straining. He had an erection.

Unbelievable. He ran a hand over his face, drew several deep breaths. His stomach slowly began to unknot.

The covers were tangled about his legs and he felt like he'd been in a furnace he was so hot. The dream, and his reaction to it, made no sense, and even if in some twisted way it did, he shied away from probing the reasons. He didn't want to know what it meant, didn't want to dwell on the strange things Virginia made him feel. Kelsey was the one who was pregnant, and Dillon planned to do only what he had to do. He would save his brother, protect Virginia, but he wouldn't touch her. So there was no chance of the dream coming true.

Still, he felt a drip of sweat slide down his brow.

The bedside alarm continued its shrill call, and feeling drugged, Dillon reached for it. He glanced at the face of the clock. It wasn't quite five a.m. and he had to meet Virginia at six. Today was the day.

His heart still thundered from the dream—which hadn't been a dream at all but rather a damned nightmare. Dillon ran a hand through his hair, shoving it away from his face.

Peddling his legs, he kicked the blankets to the end of the bed and let the cold winter morning air wash over his naked body. The sweat dried quickly and he chilled as he considered what was on his agenda.

He was going to kidnap Virginia Johnson.

Ever since the break-in he'd tried to think of another way to do things, another way to protect her *and* his brother. But he'd come up blank, without a single alternative. She refused to take the time away from the office, refused to listen to reason or take extra precautions. He'd come up with only one solution.

And his stomach had been in knots ever since.

Anyone who'd met Virginia for more than two minutes would know how she'd react to being held prisoner.

Everything in her would rebel. Hell, he'd had to fight her tooth and nail just to get the alarm installed at her home yesterday. He'd hired the very best agency, interviewed them himself, selected the alarm. Virginia had been outraged, only grudgingly giving over to his greater experience. Dillon had made sure the system was installed that very day, in case she changed her mind.

Virginia, on the best of days, was hard-nosed and contrary and independent to a fault. She wouldn't be an easy victim, and in the normal scheme of things, with a real kidnapping, her sarcasm and sharp tongue could get her hurt. Not that he would ever hurt her. He didn't hurt women, and the very idea of harming Virginia made him ache. She'd been hurt more than enough over her lifetime.

Poor Virginia. A brother who ridiculed her to employees and a spoiled little sister who thought only of herself. No wonder she'd become such a tough woman. She'd had to to survive the jackals, the people who would use her without regret.

And now he would be no better.

All his life he'd thought there were only two kinds of families. The type he and his father had, that existed on guts and strength and commitment. Their lives centered on survival, and they watched each other's backs, because they only had each other. Their bonds ran deep with the bare bones of necessity.

Then there was the other kind, the one filled with love and tenderness. Children playing, dogs barking, barbecues in the backyard and family outings to the amusement park.

Now he realized there were many kinds, because Virginia didn't fit into either group. She was as strong as an iron spike, but she didn't have the respect and dedication from her family that same trait would have earned for a man.

Neither did she have the love or tenderness. Maybe none of that even existed. Maybe it was just something he'd conjured in his brain when things had been hard and he'd foolishly tried to imagine the life he would have had with a mother. He was damn lucky his father had stuck by him, lucky the man had seen fit to teach him how to get by in the world.

Dillon glanced at the clock again. In one hour he'd be picking up Virginia. She would be expecting a day full of intimacy. He was going to give her the fright of her life. More than anything, he'd like to simply walk away, to forget Virginia and her damn dysfunctional family. The ridiculous dream that couldn't mean anything, no matter how it made his guts churn, was just that, a dream. He didn't, *wouldn't*, care for her, but for some damn reason, he wanted her. And he wanted to protect her. Chemistry, unaccountable and indisputable.

It wouldn't be easy, not with the complications growing every day, but he'd manage. Once Virginia was safely stowed away, he could concentrate on Wade.

He wondered if Cliff was using Virginia's distraction with the embezzlement to try to hurt her, to drive her away from the company. He hadn't heard Virginia mention the embezzlement, so she might not even be aware of Cliff's treachery. Or maybe she had gotten too close to discovering her brother's underhanded tactics. Virginia took her obligations to the company very seriously; she wouldn't put up with falsifying evidence. Was Cliff afraid of her finding out?

Either way, Dillon knew in his guts that Virginia was threatened. And he knew Cliff would be closing in on Wade very soon now. They couldn't have much time left. He had to get into the files and find the real embezzler before it was too late. Taking Virginia was the only option open to him, the only way to settle both problems at one time.

Virginia wouldn't like it, wouldn't understand his motives. But Wade would. He knew it had to be now or never. He had no choice. Just as his father had watched out for him, he now watched out for Wade, regardless of personal feelings or conflicts. That much, at least, he understood about family.

With cold resolution he climbed from the bed and headed for the shower.

VIRGINIA COULDN'T HELP but be excited. She'd arrived at the parking lot fifteen minutes early. It was dark and cold and everything was covered in ice. The world sparkled beneath street lamps and moonlight, looking new and clean and magical.

Headlights curved into the lot and then blinded her as they slowly crept her way. Her heartbeat picked up rhythm, and she closed her eyes, trying to calm herself. Somehow, she knew Dillon wouldn't be like the other men. He wouldn't be satisfied with half measures and fumbling in the dark. The thought shook her, but in a small part of herself that she'd kept hidden for so very long, she was excited by the notion. She felt sexy.

Absurd, a woman her age, with her weight problems and practical outlook on life, but she couldn't help it. She'd even worn sexy underclothes. A silk teddy, garters and silk hose. Instead of twisting her hair into a tight knot, she'd left it looser, more like the romantic Gibson-girl style. Little curls fell around her ears. She'd felt silly when she looked in the mirror, but she didn't redo it.

She wore a long winter-white cashmere tunic and skirt, with ankle boots of the same creamy color. Even her thick cape was a matching off-white. Her red hair was the only color. And the blush on her cheeks.

The vehicle that pulled alongside her, facing the opposite direction, wasn't the same car Dillon had kissed her in the other night. No, this was a big, mean, ugly truck. She squinted through the driver's side window and saw Dillon step out, holding on to the truck door because of the ice. He'd parked so close only a few feet separated them. He reached out and opened her door.

"Be careful. It's like a frozen pond out here. Nothing but ice."

She put her gloved hand in his and carefully stepped out. He held her securely, protectively.

For a moment she allowed it, and then she realized what she was doing, how she was being treated, and she pulled back.

All day yesterday Dillon had hovered over her. He'd fretted, much like a mother hen, and she knew it was because he was worried. The break-in, though no big deal to Virginia, had upset him. Despite his capabilities, he was a mild-mannered man in most instances, and she supposed the circumstances might be unsettling to someone without her constitution.

In a way she thought it was sweet that he'd been so concerned for her welfare. But being independent had become second nature to her. It was her greatest protective instinct. "I'm fine. Just let me open my trunk and get my bag."

"Your bag?"

Flustered, she fiddled with her car door. "You can't expect me to spend the entire day with you and not have…other stuff with me. I didn't know if we'd go out for dinner, or if you'd just want to…stay in the room." Her voice trailed off. She'd packed things to refix her hair, anticipating that it might get rather mussed, and she'd brought something sexy to wear for him when they went to bed, as well as a cocktail dress. She'd never before planned a rendezvous and wasn't certain of the protocol. But she had no intention of explaining all that to him.

"It's not important, Dillon. Just let me—"

"No. I've got it." He took her arm and, still holding on to his own door, pulled her toward his truck. "Just slide in on this side. I wouldn't want you to fall and bruise anything."

"I might fall, but you wouldn't? Does being male give you better coordination?"

In the dim light, she saw him close his eyes, saw his breath puff out in a sigh. "Virginia, if I fall, I don't care. And I can guarantee I'd be landing on a lot more solid muscle that you would."

She didn't know if that was a slur or not, but she didn't ask him to clarify because she didn't really want to know. Handing him the keys, she looked away and mumbled, "Fine. Suit yourself."

He tugged her close as she tried to slide past him. His forehead dropped to hers. "Virginia."

This close, she could see the dark sweep of his lashes, feel the warmth of his breath. He smiled. "You have an incredibly sexy ass. You know that, don't you?"

Her heart tripped with the rough compliment. He sounded sincere, and she peeked up at him. He looked sincere—and as if he was waiting for her acknowledgment of the fact. "You have a wonderful way with words."

His beautiful mouth tipped in a crooked grin, and once again his lashes swept his cheeks. "Sorry. Was my language too…colorful? I hope you won't mind. I don't know a lot of pretty words. But I do know a pretty bottom when I see one." His firm palm went to that area and gently squeezed.

She was eternally grateful for the darkness hiding her blush. As it was, he probably felt the heat from her that seemed to pulse beneath her skin. Sex talk was new to her. And the raw, spontaneous way in which Dillon spoke was far from the practiced lines she usually heard.

She tightened her lips and tried not to laugh. "Thank you."

His gaze lingered over a curl trailing past her cheek. "I like your new hairdo, too. Did you wear it this way for me?" His hand moved back to her waist.

Ironically, he didn't look at all pleased by the notion. A more sophisticated man wouldn't have asked. He would have assumed, and maybe been flattered, but he wouldn't have embarrassed the woman by mentioning it. Virginia started to reply, but Dillon interrupted her.

His eyes were narrowed, and he looked reluctant to speak, but the words emerged anyway, low and raw. "Do you let it loose when you make love?" His gloved fingertips slid over her cheek, then over the upsweep of her hair. His gaze followed the path of his hand. "How long is it?"

Oh my. How could she possibly regain control if his every word made her mute with anticipation? Dillon lowered his head and kissed her. His fingers tightened on her skull and the kiss gradually grew more intimate until his mouth ate at hers, voracious and invading. Her fingers wrapped over his wrists, not to pull him away, but to hang on. His passion made her almost dizzy. It wasn't what she was used to. He was too unrestrained, too natural, too much man. The thought made her heart jump.

He drew back slowly, in small degrees, his tongue licking her lips, his teeth nipping. Finally, his forehead rested against hers and she felt the cool, soft sweep of his long hair over her cheek. His sigh fogged the air between them. "Get in the car. I'll throw your bag in the back and we can get out of here."

Virginia glanced into the back of the battered truck and saw that the bed was covered by a tarp. "Whose truck is this?"

"Mine. It gets better traction in the snow." He opened the trunk of her car, pulled out a small overnight case and cautiously picked his way back across the ice. He stowed the bag beneath the tarp while Virginia watched, then he carefully checked to see that her car was locked up tight. She held out her hand for her keys, but he'd already shoved them deep into his jeans pocket.

"Dillon..."

"In you go, honey." Not giving her a chance to comment on his high-handedness, he lifted her off her feet, then unceremoniously dropped her into the truck.

He slid in beside her and locked the door.

Virginia fumed. "Don't you *ever* do anything like that again!"

He didn't answer, disconcerting her with his silence. In fact, he seemed different; the very air seemed different. Somehow charged. He put the truck in gear and began pulling away. She heard ice and snow crunching beneath the tires, even over the sound of the blowing heater.

She shifted in her seat, nervousness creeping in on her by slow degrees. Speaking her mind always helped her overcome her fears, helped her to reassert herself, to regain control of any situa-

tion. She'd learned that trick while still in high
school, throwing student bullies who would pick
on her about her weight into a stupor with her
blunt honesty and virulent daring. She'd em-
ployed her skill throughout college and in the
family business after her parents' deaths. So hitting people broadside with arrogant bravado
earned their dislike? It also earned their grudg-
ing obedience. And that had been good enough
for her, because through most of her life, she'd
needed every advantage she could gain. Cliff
was the oldest and the heir; Kelsey was the
baby—the sweet, *pretty one.*

Virginia filled the distressing spot of chubby
middle child.

She huffed to herself and tightened her cape
around her, regretting the brief stroll down
memory's bumpy lane. Such thoughts always
brought up her defensive feelings and the feeling
of loneliness. Only, she wasn't alone now, and
what always worked for her would work at this
moment.

She turned in her seat to face Dillon and prepared to blast him with a few facts of life, namely
that she was still the boss and as such, due all
courtesies.

"Put on your seat belt."

Of all the nerve! Her spine went rigid and her
nostrils flared. "If you don't stop ordering me
around, we can just forget this little escapade al-
together!"

Jaw clenched, he reached for the center floor-
boards of the truck, where a small thermos sat in
a molded plastic car caddy so it wouldn't tip and

spill. Two lidded cups, already filled, were beside it.

"Here." He handed her a cup. "I thought you might like something hot to keep you comfortable on the trip. I got you out of bed so early I wasn't sure if you'd have time for coffee at home."

He glanced at her, and she knew he was judging her mood, trying to decide if he'd managed to placate her. She still felt affronted, but accepted that he was trying. And in a small way, his take-charge attitude stimulated her. In a *very* small way.

"Thank you."

He smiled, looking dramatically relieved, then he made a teasing face. "If I ask nice, will you also put on your seat belt? These roads are like a skating rink, and I don't want to take any chances with you."

She rather liked his teasing, and his concern. She smiled as she buckled her belt. "There. Happy?"

"Yes." He reached over and, fingers spread wide, put his large hand on her thigh, gripping her in a familiar way. She held her breath and her stomach flipped sweetly. She waited to see what he would do next, but he seemed preoccupied by the deserted road, almost distracted. An occasional street lamp or passing car lit the interior of the truck cab and she saw his gloved hand looking wickedly dark and sinful against the pale material of her skirt. He didn't move, didn't speak. But that heavy hand remained on her leg, and she was incredibly aware of it, of him. She wondered if that hadn't been his intention all along.

She sipped her coffee, then cleared her throat. "Would you like your cup?"

"In a little while."

"Where exactly are we going?"

He flashed her a look she couldn't read, then his gaze dropped to the cup she held. "It's a surprise." He returned his attention to the road.

She didn't want to spoil the adventure, but his strange mood put her on edge. She'd survived a long time by trusting her hunches, and right now, it felt as if things weren't aligned quite properly. She never felt like this about men, and they never acted like this around her. Always, Dillon had gone out of his way to speak with her, to turn on the charm. But now he seemed so distant, sitting there in a manner that felt very *expectant.*

Did he want something of her? Was she supposed to be doing something? If so, she didn't know what. Dillon didn't behave like other men, which was both exciting and a bit unsettling.

She continued to sip her coffee, trying to push the mingled uneasiness and anticipation away.

After a moment, they turned onto a deserted southbound expressway, heading for Kentucky. Virginia hadn't gotten enough sleep, so the silence, combined with the easy driving and the early-morning darkness made her eyelids heavy. She closed her eyes and rested her head against the seat. "Where are we going, Dillon?"

His hand left her thigh to rub softly over her

cheek, then around her ear. "You look like a snow bunny, you know that?"

His words were so soft. They drifted over her like his lazily moving fingers. With considerable effort, she forced her eyes open and turned her head in his direction. "I wanted to look nice for you," she whispered, then closed her eyes again, wondering where in hell that bit of confession had come from. She held tightly to her coffee and sipped. The mug was almost empty, but that was okay; she didn't want any more. She wanted to sleep.

She heard Dillon sigh. "I'm so sorry, Virginia. Remember that, okay?"

Something wasn't making sense. He sounded pained, but somehow determined. She frowned and forced her eyes open again. Everything was blurred and it took her precious seconds to focus again. Dillon kept glancing at her curiously, his brow furrowed, his gaze intent and diamond hard.

Suddenly, she knew. Her chest tightened in panic and she stared at him. Her breath came fast. "You bastard. *You poisoned me.*"

"Not poison," he said, but his voice was strained and there was a ringing in her ears. None of it made sense, at least, in no way she wanted to contemplate. She wouldn't let the fear take her, wouldn't let him take her. Hadn't he warned her himself that someone was threatening her? But he'd been with her when the intruder had been in her house. Unless they were working together...

She narrowed her eyes on him and saw his

worried frown. They were moving quickly down the expressway, too quickly. Farther and farther from home. The roads were empty, the day still dark and cold. She felt weaker by the second, and she fought it. She'd have to use her wits before they deserted her. Later, when she was safe, she'd let the hurt consume her. But not until she was safe—and alone once again.

DILLON WISHED SHE'D say something, anything, rather than stare at him in that accusing way. It reminded him of the dream and his stomach cramped. She had to be frightened, and he hated doing this to her. Nevertheless, his body was tense, prepared for whatever she might try.

"What have you done to me?"

He felt cold inside. "I drugged you, just as you assumed. It's a sleeping drug. It won't hurt you. Even now, you're getting drowsy. You might as well stop fighting it, Virginia." More than anything, he wanted her to sleep so he wouldn't have to see the disgust and mistrust in her eyes.

She shook her head as if to clear it. "Where are we?"

"Nowhere yet." He pulled off the main highway and onto a less-traveled rural route, slowing the truck accordingly. It would take longer this way, but there wasn't likely to be any traffic at all. "We've got a while to go."

Her head lolled on the back of the seat, and she looked out the windows at the scrubby trees, the endless snow. Dillon knew what she saw; no one had cleared this area, and the road was almost invisible between the trees lining it.

It had turned bitterly cold, and the wind whistled around the truck. He saw Virginia shiver and rub her eyes and a strange tenderness welled up in his chest. "Honey, don't be afraid, okay?"

"Ha! I'm fine," she managed to snap in slurred tones. She held her shoulders stiff and her hands clenched in her lap. He knew she was fighting the drug and her fear with everything she had. But it was useless.

"As soon as we get to the cabin and you're awake, I'll explain what's going on. I don't want you to worry."

"I'm thirsty," she whispered, ignoring his speech. He supposed, given the circumstances, his assurances *were* bizarre.

"Sure. Here, there's a little coffee left." She glared at him and he added, "Mine. This isn't drugged. See?" He lifted the mug to this mouth to demonstrate, and that's when she hit him.

He should have seen it coming, but he hadn't realized she still had that much strength. Her doubled fists smacked into the cup, jamming it into his mouth, cutting his lip and clipping his nose. He cursed, dropping the cup and doing his best to steer the truck safely to the side of the road. He hit the brakes and shifted gears. They spun to a rocky stop after sliding several feet.

Already, Virginia was working on her door. He'd locked it, of course, and she fumbled, crying in frustration as she tried to find the way to unlock it. He'd put a large piece of electrical tape over the lock switch, just in case.

His hands closed on her shoulders and she turned on him, twisting in the seat and kicking wildly with her small boots. She hit him in the thigh and he grunted.

Subduing her without hurting her proved damn difficult. He finally just gave up and threw his entire weight on top of her. She gasped and cried and cursed as he captured both her hands and held them over her head. His chest pressed against her breasts, his thighs pinned hers.

"Virginia, shh. Baby, it's all right."

She looked up, and stark fear darkened her blurry eyes, cutting him deeply.

"Aw, damn." He closed his eyes, trying to gather his wits. "Honey, I swear, I'm not going to hurt you. Please believe me."

"Then why?" She began to struggle again, but she was weaker now, her eyelids only half-open. He lowered his chest, forcing her to gasp for air, to go completely still.

"I promise I'll explain everything at the cabin."

"What cabin?" she cried, the words slurred and raw.

"The cabin where I'm going to keep you for just a few days, until I'm sure it's safe. Now, can I let you go?"

She stared up at him, blinking slowly, still fighting. "Your lip is bleeding. And your nose is turning blue."

"I think you might have broken it." He tried a

small grin, but with his lip numb, it might not have been too effective. "You pack a hell of a punch, especially for a drugged lady."

"I don't understand you. You're not the man I thought I knew."

"No, I don't suppose I am. But I won't hurt you. And in a few days, I'll take you home. Okay?"

Slowly, she nodded, and when he cautiously released her, she dropped her head back on the seat and took several deep breaths. After a moment, she pulled herself upright. It seemed to take a great deal of effort, but he didn't touch her. He didn't want her to slug him again, or possibly hurt herself jerking away.

Her gaze went to the door and the electrical tape. "I should have noticed."

"It was dark." He dabbed at his split lip with a hankie. Thankfully, his nose felt more bruised than broken, but it still hurt like hell.

"I have to use the bathroom."

That stymied him for just a moment. He lifted his hands. "There's nothing for miles, no gas station, no restaurants…"

"I need to go now. I can't wait."

He measured the wisdom of letting her out, but then he looked at her face. He wanted more than anything for her to trust him just a bit. He frowned at his own weakness. "All right. But stay right beside the truck. I'll turn my back."

She swallowed and her face flamed. To Dillon, she look remarkably appealing and feminine. Her hair was half-undone, long strands tumbling around her shoulders, waving around her face. Her strange topaz eyes were slumberous, filled with a mixture of muted anger and anxiety. She breathed heavily, slowly, her lush breasts rising and falling. He hated her fear, hated being the cause of it. But he hadn't had a choice.

Icy wind and wet snow assaulted him as he opened the door and stepped out. He turned and reached in for Virginia. She swayed, then offered him her hand to allow him to help her out on the driver's side. That was his first clue. Virginia never admitted to needing help with anything or from anyone. She especially wouldn't do so now, while she felt so angry and betrayed.

The realization hit just before she did. This time her aim was for his groin, and her aim was true, though thankfully not as solid as it might have been, given her lethargic state.

Air left his lungs in a whoosh and he bent double, then dropped to his knees in the icy snow. He ground his teeth against the pain and cursed her—the stubborn, deceiving little cat. This time when he got his hands on her...

Virginia tried to run, but her legs weren't working right. She was clumsy, stumbling and falling again and again. She headed for the scraggly trees, even though they wouldn't offer a speck of concealment. Dillon forced himself to his feet, leaning on the truck as he watched her. She moved awkwardly, hampered by her fear, the drug and the thick snow. He took one more deep breath, which didn't do a damn thing for the lingering pain and nausea, and started off in a lope after her.

She must have heard his pursuit because she turned to stare wildly at him—and tripped. Dillon saw her go down, saw her land heavily on the ground and not get back up. His heart stopped, then began to thud against his ribs. Oh God.

"Virginia!" He forgot his own pain and charged to her. She lay limp, her face in the snow, and he fell to his knees beside her. She didn't move. He gently lifted her head and felt for a lump of any kind. There was nothing; the snow had cushioned her fall.

She opened her eyes the tiniest bit and glared at him. In a mere whisper, she said, "You're a miserable jerk, Dillon."

"I know, baby. I know." He smoothed the silky red hair away from her face while cradling her in his arms. "Easy, now. It's all right. How do you feel?"

"You've drugged me." Her head lolled, her words almost incoherent.

"It'll be all right, Virginia. I promise. I would never hurt you."

He heard a low, weak cry, and knew the sound came from Virginia. "Shh. It's all right. I swear it's all right." He listened to his ridiculous litany and wanted to curse himself. Nothing was all right, and he had the feeling it might never be again.

He cuddled her close to his chest, rocked her. "Just relax and go to sleep, sweetheart. I'll take care of everything. I'll take care of you. That's all I'm trying to do, you know."

Her eyes shut and her body went limp. But just before she gave in, before she let him have his way, she whispered, "You never really wanted me at all." She sighed. "You never wanted me. Damn you, Dillon...damn you, you never wanted..."

He listened to her breathing. She was asleep. Deeply asleep. Quickly, the cold slicing through him, he hefted her into his arms and started back for the truck. His groin ached and his nose throbbed, but that was nothing compared with how his heart hurt.

For Virginia's own safety, he wouldn't take any more chances. She had proven to be a creative captive, and he knew she'd fight him tooth and nail if he gave her the opportunity. That meant taking certain precautions that she wasn't going to like.

For the second time that day, he lifted her into his truck. But as he strapped her in, as he looked around to make certain there were no witnesses, his brain played her words over and over again. *You never wanted me.*

SHE WAS SO WRONG, so damn wrong. He wanted her more than he'd ever wanted any woman. And it made no sense. He didn't like her family or her problems or the confusion she made him feel.

She'd passed out cursing him. Typical of Virginia to fade out while raising hell.

He smoothed his hand over her head, which lay in his lap, her cheek against his expanding fly. He knew it was only his imagination, but he thought he could feel the soft warmth of her breath there.

He was a sick bastard, kidnapping a woman and then getting aroused over her sleeping body. But he couldn't help himself. Everything about her excited him, and he was helpless against her. He wouldn't violate her, never that. But he had taken advantage. He was the one who'd pulled her so close. And even as he drove, trying his damnedest to distance himself from what he'd done, he was pulling the pins from her hair and smoothing it with his fingers. He'd told himself he only meant to make her more comfortable, but he knew it was a lie.

Her flaming hair now lay thick and full and shiny over his lap and his belly and his thighs. He shuddered, feeling in his mind and body how it would be if he and Virginia were naked. He tangled a fist in the sinfully sexy mass and pulled it carefully away from her face.

Thick brown lashes lay over her pale cheeks, her lips slightly parted, all arrogance and dominance washed away. She didn't look like a virago or a witch. She was simply an incredibly enticing woman. But he knew better, and he could only imagine how she'd react when she awoke. It would be a while yet. She'd been sleeping for only an hour. Still, he hadn't given her that much of the drug, just enough to make certain she couldn't figure out where they'd gone. He hadn't wanted her to know where they'd be staying.

The sun was trying to show itself on this hazy winter morning and they'd almost reached their destination when he felt her fingers move, clasping weakly at his thigh. She made a small moaning sound and he stilled. He wanted her to sleep just a little longer. There was one more thing he had to do—one more precaution to take—once they reached the cabin, and it would be easier for both of them if Virginia slept through it.

Because he knew without a single doubt, Virginia would never willingly give up her clothes.

He didn't plan to give her a choice.

6

Virginia opened her eyes and accepted the feeling of dread that swirled around her. Cautiously, not sure what was wrong or why she felt so disoriented, she lay perfectly still and peered at her surroundings. Her head pounded as she took in the rough plank walls and bare floor. She was in a narrow bed piled high with quilts, cozy and warm, but the air on her face was cool. The cabin, or more like a shack, didn't appear to have modern conveniences, but the fireplace across the room blazed brightly, the flames licking high and casting an orange glow over the otherwise dark room.

Memories returned in bits and pieces, and with them came a deep ache in her heart. She closed her eyes and bit her lips as the emotional pain swelled.

That rotten, deceiving conniver. That miserable creep. He'd kidnapped her! He'd played her for a fool, pretending to want her, when in truth it had all been a game. She opened her eyes and willed away the tears that threatened. Virginia Johnson did not cry.

After taking several uncertain breaths, she worked up the nerve to turn her head and look for Dillon. She didn't see him anywhere. The

minuscule cabin had only one separate room, not
much bigger than a closet. Through its open door
she could see it was a bathroom, butting up next
to the kitchen area. There was one narrow
counter, a stove, small freezer and refrigerator
situated around a metal sink. The cabin's one
and only window, mostly blocked by snow on
the outside, was situated over the sink.

There were two chairs, one a wooden rocker,
the other a threadbare armchair, facing the fireplace. The bed she was lying in—a cot, really—
hugged the back wall. Beside the cot was a small
dresser that served as a nightstand, holding a
clock and a tiny lamp with no shade. In the middle of the room was a badly scarred pine table
and two matching chairs.

There was no sound other than the snapping
and hissing of the fire. She swallowed, wondering if she might have a chance to escape.

Damn the cold and the snow and whatever
distance they'd covered. She would not accept
being a victim without choices. It didn't matter to
her if she had to run all the way home.

But as she cautiously sat up in the bed and the
quilts fell to her lap, she realized something that
had escaped her notice thus far.

Dillon had taken all her clothes.

She stared, appalled, at her barely covered
breasts. She had on her teddy, thank God, but
other than that, she was as bare as the day she'd
been born. Her nipples, stiff now with the washing of cold air, could be plainly seen through the
material. Her nylons were even gone, but it
didn't matter.

Mortification hit her first. He'd removed her clothes! He'd viewed her imperfect body, no doubt in minute detail. He'd looked at her at his leisure and found the evidence of her extra pounds—her rounded hips and thighs, the softness of her belly, the fullness of her breasts. She wondered if he'd chuckled as he stripped off her clothes; had he been amused by her attempt at seductiveness?

She felt queasy, sick with embarrassment. Her face flamed and her vision blurred. It was more than a woman could accept, more than she could bear.

Thankfully, outrage hit next, bringing with it a bloodcurdling scream of rage that erupted from her throat and resounded through the tiny cabin again and again.

The door crashed open and Dillon came charging in, his body strangely balanced as if for battle, his gaze alert as he made a quick, thorough survey of the room. He held himself in a fighter's stance, his black gaze steely and bright. Virginia could only stare.

Oh my. Closing her mouth slowly, she looked him over. He'd shed his civilized demeanor and hadn't left behind a single trace. His long hair, held off his face by a red bandanna rolled and tied around his forehead, gave him a pagan appearance. The bruise shadowing his nose and the corner of his mouth, discolored even through his sun-browned skin, added to the impression of savagery. His jeans were faded and torn, displaying a part of one muscular thigh and two bare knees. The material over his fly was soft and

white with age and cupped him lovingly. His
heavy coat was gone, and his flannel shirt lay
open at the throat, the sleeves rolled high over a
gray thermal shirt. Incredibly, he seemed to be
sweating.

His black eyes lit on her, then perused her
body, lingering on her throbbing breasts and the
shadowed juncture of her legs. Belatedly, Virginia grabbed the quilt and snatched it to her
throat. Her insides seemed to curl up tight.

"What's wrong?" he demanded.

Virginia stared at him. His chest heaved from
whatever activity had made him sweat, and possibly the fright she'd given him. She realized that
he must have come charging in prepared to rescue her from some unknown threat. She wanted
to laugh—after all, he was her only threat—but
she couldn't manage it.

When she remained mute, he firmed his
mouth into a grim line and headed back to close
the door he'd left hanging open. "Stupid question, right? Do you always screech like a wet cat
when you wake up?"

She was taken aback by his uncharacteristic
sarcasm, and it took her a moment to gather the
wit to speak. "Where the hell are my clothes?"

"Gone."

That flat answer caused her heart to skip in
dread. "What do you mean, gone? Damn it, Dillon, what's going on here?"

He walked over and sat on the edge of the cot,
prompting her to scurry back as far as she could.
The wall felt cold against her shoulder blades,
but the alternative would have been to touch

him, and that was out of the question. She could already smell him—a cold, fresh-air scent mixed with raw masculinity and clean sweat. His dark eyes had never looked more intense as he took his time gazing at her features.

In a low, awe-filled voice, he asked, "How the hell did you manage to hide so much hair in that tight little knot you usually wear?" His gaze followed the length of one long curl as it rippled over her shoulder, almost to her lap. Words beyond her, Virginia squirmed under his scrutiny.

He reached out and twined a thick strand around his finger. "I've never seen hair like yours."

Virginia jerked, then winced at the tug on her hair. Dillon released her.

He chewed the side of his mouth, all the while studying her. "I was outside chopping wood. I meant to be in here when you woke up so you wouldn't be frightened. But as you can see, the only heat we're going to have here is from the fireplace and stove."

"Let me go."

"No." He pulled the bandanna off and used it to wipe his face. His long hair fell free and she caught another whiff of that enticing scent unique to him. "After I finish splitting the wood, I'll put on some soup or something and you can eat. I'll have you comfortable soon enough."

No longer was he the man she knew. He didn't act or move or speak like the old Dillon. There was no feigned deference, no show of politeness. He told her what he would do, and seemed to think she'd simply accept it.

But her mind shied away from that, from the ramifications of being stolen away by a man she didn't know—*this* man. So she skipped the questions clamoring uppermost in her mind and concentrated on another, more immediate one. "Where are my clothes, you bastard."

He made a tsking sound, amusement bright in his eyes. "Such language, and from a lady of your standing."

Without thought, she swung at him, her burst of anger overshadowing her better judgment. When he caught her fist, he was grinning with genuine humor. "I can't tell you how relieved I am you're not wailing and crying and shivering in fear." He moved, flipping her down on the bed and catching her other fist, too, as she swung it. He leaned over her, his big body hot and hard, covering her own. In a whisper, he said, "Don't fight me, Virginia. You can't win."

His gaze bore into hers, and he was so close she felt his every breath. Then, suddenly, he sat up and moved away. The racing of her heart and the jumping of her stomach refused to subside. She didn't move, too intent on trying to calm herself from what felt like a tussle with a large male animal. Which wasn't far from the truth.

He caught a chair from the table and swung it around, straddling it so he could face her. "I took your clothes so you won't try running off again. I can't let you hurt yourself, and that's exactly what would happen if you tried to escape me."

Slowly, keeping a watchful eye on him, she sat back up and rearranged the quilt to cover her body. "What would you do to me if I tried?"

Deep dimples creased his sun-bronzed cheeks as he laughed. "I don't intend to do anything to you."

The words, combined with his misplaced humor, hurt more than she wanted to admit. Virginia lifted her chin. "Of course I realize now that you never wanted me, that pretending to want me was only a nasty little scam to fool me. That's not what I meant."

The humor left as quickly as it had appeared. "We're a long way from anything," he said, biting off the words. "There's nothing but ice and snow and freezing cold out there. If you tried to find your way home or find help, you'd never make it. The snow has gotten worse, burying all the roads. Taking your clothes was just a way to discourage you from even trying."

"I won't run, I promise. Just give me my clothes."

He eyed her, his gaze drifting lazily over her face. "I know you, Virginia. I know how your mind works. You'll try to run because sitting here doing nothing is the one thing you won't be able to abide."

"Yes, you know me so well," she sneered, wanting to hurt him the way he'd hurt her. But she couldn't because he didn't actually care about her. He never had. "You've been working on this plan for a long time, haven't you? When exactly did you come up with the idea?"

"To kidnap you? After the break-in at your house."

"Ha! Can't you be honest even now? Do you

expect me to think you were *ever* sincere, that anything between us has *ever* been real?"

His gaze never faltered, but she saw his hands tighten into fists, saw the muscles of his shoulders bunch. "I got myself hired on at the company and talked you into coming away with me, all for a single purpose."

Knowing it and actually hearing it were too different things. She fought back the lump that formed in her throat and tried not to sound as wounded as she felt. "That's what I figured. What an idiot I've been."

He cursed and she jumped at the sound. "You're not an idiot, Virginia. I'm just very good at what I do."

"Lying, you mean?"

His look was quelling. "You know that's not what I meant."

"Then what?"

He shook his head and she knew the subject was closed. "Are you hungry? Or do you want something to drink?"

"And have you poison me again? No, thanks. Maybe next time you'll kill me."

He growled and came off his chair with a burst of energy. Pushing long fingers through his hair, he paced away from her, then jerked back around to face her, his expression fierce. "I'm not going to hurt you. Just the opposite, damn it. I'm trying to keep you safe."

"Oh?" She raised one eyebrow, deliberately egging him on. Somewhere, deep inside, she refused to be truly afraid of him. She'd spent better than two weeks getting to know him, and she couldn't believe her intuition had been so flawed. She refused to accept that she could have made such an enormous error. But she was hurt. Very hurt. And that made her almost blind with anger. "I suppose I should accept the word of a kidnapper? A pervert?"

He propped his hands on lean hips and his jaw worked. "I am not a pervert."

"You stole my clothes while I was unconscious!" She still couldn't bear the thought of it. "You...you looked at me! That's the lowest, most despicable..."

He stalked closer and bent low until he was nose to nose with her. "I'll take the rest of your damn clothes with you wide-awake if you don't stop trying to provoke me!"

Again, she cowered, wondering why she'd ever wanted a man who would stand up to her. Right now, she'd gladly trade Dillon for a man who would do her bidding.

The look on his face and the set of his body told her there'd be no swaying him. She swallowed and wisely decided against saying anything that might agitate him further.

Dillon shook his head in disgust. He straightened and took a small step away from the cot. "Damn it, I don't want to yell at you. I don't want to frighten you."

"Could've fooled me," she muttered, forgetting herself again while still keeping watch on him.

His head dropped forward and he laughed. "Ah, Virginia, you just don't know when to quit, do you?" He scrubbed both hands over his face, then raised his gaze to her again. He no longer laughed, but his smile lingered. He shook his head when he saw how he'd confused her. "You're a unique woman, you know that?"

The softly spoken words wiggled down deep into her heart, and she almost choked on her bitterness. She would *not* play the fool again. "Are you forgetting, Dillon, that the game is over? There's no reason for you to continue to flatter me with your nonsense. I've already been duped. Your plan succeeded."

He sat back in his chair with a deep sigh. "Would you like to know what the plan actually is, or are you happier to sit there and bitch?"

Virginia felt the words like a slap and she scowled. "How dare you?"

"What? Are you going to fire me?" He laughed again. "Grow up, Virginia. We're on new ground now. You'll find I can dare to do whatever I choose."

Her pulse fluttered in dread, but Dillon just made a sound of disgust. "Now don't go rounding those big gold eyes at me. I'm not going to hurt you. I've already told you that."

"You're threatening me," she said indignantly.

"Not at all. Just trying to explain to you what I have in mind."

Virginia tightened her hold on the quilt and glared at him. "Well, you can save your breath, because I already figured it out."

"Is that so?" He waved an encouraging hand at her. "So tell me, Virginia. What have you deduced in that quick little mind of yours?"

"You want money. But that's plain stupid, and I hadn't figured you for stupid." She looked him over with as much contempt as she could muster, then added, "A criminal, maybe, but not a stupid one. Surely you realize there's no love lost between me and Cliff. In fact, he detests me. I won't be surprised if he refuses to pay you a single penny. He'll probably be glad to be rid of me."

"That's part of what had me so worried, truth to tell," he admitted, his words sharp and filled with anger.

"Ah, that bothers you doesn't it? You're stuck with me and there's no way to collect. Now what'll you do?"

Very deliberately, he stood and put his chair back at the table. As he retied the bandanna around his forehead, she watched the flexing of his biceps and the bunching muscles of his forearms and thick wrists.

"Virginia?"

Her gaze shot back to his glaring face and she reddened, knowing he'd caught her staring.

"I think I'll save the conversation for later. If I stay in here and listen to you go on, I might be tempted to violence."

"Ha! You said you wouldn't hurt me. Are you a liar as well as a kidnapper and a pervert?" She silently cursed the words once they'd left her mouth, but right now, words were all she had. She felt defenseless and vulnerable and emotionally wounded. She hated it. She almost hated him.

Dillon headed for the door. "No, I'm not a liar.

And I won't hurt you. At least, not the way you're implying. But if I hear you putting yourself down like that again, I will turn you over my knee. And trust me, you won't enjoy the experience." As he opened the door he looked at her over his shoulder, and his black gaze lingered on her hips. "Although, considering what you've put me through these past weeks, I think *I'd* probably enjoy every second of it."

The door slammed closed behind him and Virginia let out her breath. Good grief, she felt scorched by that look and the words that had accompanied it. Put herself down? Was that what she'd been doing? And why should he care anyway?

Dillon wasn't the man she'd believed him to be. He definitely wasn't the meek, considerate lover she expected. No, Dillon would never accept half measures in the dark; she had a feeling that when he made love, he did so with the same intensity he'd just shown her. He wouldn't be *nice* about it; he'd be demanding, taking everything a woman had and giving her back just as much of himself.

Virginia shivered at the thought of making love to this new Dillon. He was hard and commanding—but for some reason, she still, ultimately, felt safe with him. At times his expression seemed foreboding, but she never feared any real harm or she wouldn't have given her mouth so much freedom. Dillon would not hurt her.

His contradictions—the way he used his strength and power with such devastating gentleness—thrilled her to the center of her feminine core. Every time he looked at her, her heart knocked against her ribs and her stomach tightened with desire.

She still wanted him, probably more than ever. But to him she was only a means to an end. For that, she would never forgive him.

She closed her eyes on a silent groan. She had to be the biggest fool alive because she wanted him anyway. Until now, she hadn't known such a need could exist. If she didn't get away from Dillon soon, she'd probably end up begging him to take her.

She couldn't let that happen.

Hawes— He'd take it to her, then to her feminine core. Dewy, damp. Her flushed skin, her . . .
He clenched his teeth and forced himself to think about . . . desserts.

She'd wanted him to think of her as a . . . tart. He wanted her only to think of relating, but that was wrong for the two of them.

7

CHOPPING WOOD PROVED to be cathartic. Dillon could release his tension, both sexual and emotional.

Seeing her sitting there, her thick mass of hair loose and silky, her heavy breasts with the large dark nipples barely restrained by her sheer lingerie, had cost him. When he'd undressed her, he'd tried to be detached. He hadn't looked any more than he had to, and he'd detested himself because he got aroused anyway.

With Virginia wide-awake and spitting venom at him, he hadn't *not* been able to look. He wanted her. He wanted her so bad he couldn't stop thinking about it. He lingered on the memory of those rounded breasts in his palms, and he wanted, at this moment, to know the taste of her nipples, to suck her and lick her and hear her moan for him.

He should have explained it all to her. That would have put her at ease, at least on one level. But she'd have been devastated to know the lengths Cliff had gone to to get rid of her. He wanted to demolish Cliff, and before this was over, he probably would.

Virginia might not believe him if he told her all his suspicions right now. She'd admitted to knowing how little Cliff cared for her, but Dillon knew she didn't think he was really capable of hurting her. She disdained Cliff, she didn't fear him.

Still, Dillon should have explained about Wade. Then maybe she wouldn't consider him a mercenary bastard driven by monetary rewards. She would have known, too, the absurdity of her charge that he didn't want her. He wanted her too damn much.

But putting some distance between them had been the most immediate necessity. He'd kidnapped her, and once this was over, he'd leave. That was an irrefutable fact. He wouldn't complicate things by giving in to his need. Throwing in the threat of a paddling had been sheer self-defense. He had to find a way to get her to stop baiting him, so he could find a way to keep his distance and do what he knew to be right. But with every word out of her mouth, she tempted him in a way no other woman had. He wanted to kiss her quiet, to prove his dominance over her, to be male to her female.

Not that he would ever raise a hand to her. His father had taught him that hurting anyone smaller or weaker than himself was a sign of true cowardice. Even worse was to hurt a woman. Females were to be protected, looked after. Just as you protected your family. Only, Virginia didn't want or need anyone to protect her. Disregarding physical strength, she was the most capable woman he'd ever met. Which meant he had no place in her life at all. What he had to give, she didn't need. And when all was said and done, she wouldn't want him around anyway.

But he wasn't going to explain his feelings to Virginia. If she feared him just a little, maybe she'd keep her insults behind her teeth and give him some peace. He enjoyed her show of defiance, but right now he needed to enjoy her a little less so he could maintain some control.

His arms loaded with firewood, he kicked the front door open. He automatically looked toward the bed, and Virginia, but she wasn't there. Only sheer instinct caused him to drop the wood and roll away a split second before a heavy frying pan came swishing past his head.

He cursed, then grabbed her bare ankles and jerked. She went down hard on her bottom, screeching curses so hot it was a wonder they didn't melt the snow. He snatched the frying pan out of her hand when she tried again to heft the damn thing toward his skull.

"*Goddammit!*" It was like wrestling with a wild woman. He did his best not to hurt her when he slammed down on top of her, using his knee to spread her bare thighs so she couldn't kick him and holding both her wrists in one tight fist. "Keep still, Virginia, before you hurt yourself!"

"You're the one hurting me, you cretin! Let me go." She thrashed and her hair whipped around her face, slapping against him.

"No." Dillon dropped his forehead to her shoulder, then quickly flinched away when she tried to sink her teeth into his neck. Clasping her chin with his free hand, he growled, "Maybe I should give you that paddling now."

"Try it and I'll emasculate you!"

So much for empty threats, he thought.

She wiggled and he felt the softness of her, the giving of her feminine body cradling his own. He clenched his jaw even as his muscles hardened and his penis followed suit. From one breath to the next he was as hard as a stone, pressing into her soft belly. "You already tried emasculating me, remember? I may never father children."

The low, husky sound of his voice gave away his dilemma, and Virginia stilled, her eyes wide on his face. In a whisper, she asked, "Criminals don't want to father children, do they?"

The absurdity of it hit him. How could this woman, whom—he kept reminding himself—he did *not* like, keep making him lose his head? It defied reason.

"Forget I said that." He pushed up, coming to his knees between her spread thighs. She gasped and struggled, but he held her wrists.

Staring hard into her eyes, he asked, "Why did you attack me?"

"Because I can't let you use me."

Despite his best intentions, Dillon gazed over her body. Her legs were sprawled around him, the teddy pulled tight to her frame, showing every curve and hollow. Damn but she was lush and rounded and generously built, the way a woman was supposed to be built. She would cushion a man with her feminine curves. He felt all that giving softness beneath him, and the feeling tempted him. Damn but it tempted him.

Forcing himself to look away from the outline of her feminine cleft, the hint of soft curls, he raised his gaze to her face. He saw her flushed cheeks and the wariness in her eyes. He understood. He himself could barely breathe. "Virginia, I have no intention of forcing myself on you. You don't have to be worried about rape."

Her mouth fell open before she narrowed her eyes and hissed, "I wasn't talking about that, you ass! I was talking about your using me in some moneymaking scheme."

She strained against his grip, and he struggled to subdue her. "In that, you have no choice." He touched her shoulder where an angry red welt had risen against her white skin. "Did I hurt you when I yanked you down?"

"This is insane!" Her voice now sounded shaky and he continued to soothe the small injury with strokes of his fingertips. "First you kidnap me and now you're concerned about giving me a bruise or two?"

"You have other bruises?"

The flush spread to her breasts and she looked away. "No, I just..."

"Show me, Virginia."

Her chest heaved and she briefly closed her eyes. "Get off me, you oaf."

When she looked at him again, he could see her embarrassment in the way she squirmed. He tilted his head, then surveyed her lush hips, remembering how hard she'd hit the floor. "Your bottom? Did I hurt you when I pulled you down?"

He could feel her trembling. "Dillon, *please*, this is ridiculous."

He released her and stood, then caught her upper arms and pulled her to her feet. He didn't like hearing her beg, didn't like seeing her fear of him. Holding her a moment longer than was necessary, he studied her downcast face, the way her hair fell like a curtain, hiding her expression and a good portion of her body. He dropped his hands and took a step away. "Get in the bed before you catch pneumonia. This floor is like ice."

Her back stiffened. "Why don't you just give me back my boots then?"

No matter how he tried, he couldn't put the thought of other bruises from his mind. He studied her, his gaze lingering again on her hips.

"Dillon?"

He shook his head. "No. I like you better just the way you are, honey."

Her beautiful eyes narrowed and she hissed a vicious curse at him.

He couldn't help but laugh, then he chucked her chin. "Face it, Virginia. Like this, you're more manageable. Now get in the bed before I put you there."

He picked up the frying pan and stepped over scattered logs as he went into the kitchen, not bothering to see if she obeyed. A moment later, he heard the cot squeak, and when he looked, Virginia was again buried beneath the quilts. She stared toward him, her expression stony.

After washing his hands, he opened the refrigerator and found a small roast. He put it on a battered old cutting board. "Cliff is charging my younger brother, Wade, with embezzlement."

Using a sharp knife—one he vowed to remember to hide after he finished his chore—Dillon cut the meat into small chunks and put them in a stew pot. "I know you had no idea Wade Sanders is my brother. Actually, we're half brothers, so our last names are different and we don't look a hell of a lot alike. We share the same mother, though I never knew the woman." He glanced at Virginia to see how she took his explanation. She watched him, blessedly silent for a change.

"Wade is innocent, of course, but since I don't know what trumped-up evidence your brother has on him, I couldn't defend him. We obviously don't have the money your family has. Taking this to court would be ludicrous. Your brother's high-priced lawyers would crucify Wade. I had to think of another plan."

He added water to the pot and lit the stove. After throwing in a chopped onion and putting on the lid, he went to the fireplace and piled on more logs. Sparks leaped out at him, then landed harmlessly on the dusty wooden floor, where they faded away.

Personally, he thought the room was already too warm, but then, he was fully clothed. And damn near fully aroused.

He glanced at Virginia. Her entire body was rigid. "This may come as a surprise, but Wade and your sister, Kelsey, are in love."

He heard her gasp and their eyes connected. He felt touched by her anxiety, but forced himself to ignore it. It was past time she got things straight.

Small logs were scattered all over the floor from where he'd dropped them when she'd attacked. He began gathering them up, more to give himself something to do than for the sake of neatness. "On top of all that, and regardless of what you think, someone is trying to hurt you. I don't know for sure who it is yet, but I have my suspicions." He wouldn't come right out and name her brother. That would serve no purpose, at least not yet.

"You're the one trying to hurt me, Dillon."

He stilled in the process of stacking the wood by the fireplace, unable to ignore her sneering tone. Without looking at her, he said, "Never. I didn't lie about that, Virginia. When this is all over, I'll take you back and then disappear. You don't have to be afraid about that."

"After you've collected your money?"

"I'm not asking for any money. I need to clear Wade. But I couldn't do that, not while I was distracted worrying about you."

She appeared to chew that over. "You said you'd leave when this is done. Where will you go?"

He shook his head. He couldn't tell her he'd be flying to Mexico, back to his home. The less she knew about him, the better. "With you out of your office, I should be able to go through some files, do some checking."

"You kidnapped me to get me out of my office? You drugged me and dragged me to this dirty little cabin in the middle of nowhere, stripped me and scared me half to death, just so you could access my files?"

She sounded appalled by such logic. She also seemed to have forgotten the fact of her own threatened circumstances. But he wouldn't remind her of that again. "Cliff hates Wade, and he's trying to railroad him. All I need is a little time to prove it."

"You could be wrong."

"No. I'm good at reading people."

"I used to think the same thing," she said with a great deal of disgust.

He went on as if she hadn't interrupted. "I've gotten to know your brother pretty well. He's a petty bastard who wants things his own way whether that's the right way or not. He objects to your involvement because it injures his pride, not because he thinks it isn't necessary. And he's accusing Wade of embezzlement because he doesn't want him involved with Kelsey, not because Wade is guilty. Cliff is insecure, and he deals with his problems in an underhanded way."

She didn't respond and Dillon cleared his throat. He didn't have it in him to force the issue of Cliff's violent tendencies right now. "Anyway, Wade and Kelsey will be married."

"No!" Virginia shot forward on the bed, her expression and tone frantic. "Kelsey is too young and—"

"And Wade isn't good enough?"

"That's not what I was going to say!" she nervously smoothed her hands over the quilt and licked her lips. "Kelsey doesn't know what she's doing. She's only twenty-two."

"Almost twenty-three, and she'd disagree with you. She thinks she knows exactly what she's doing. She claims she loves Wade. And I know he worships her. He'll take good care of her, Virginia."

"No, Dillon, please. You have to let me talk to her, reason with her. Please."

Dillon walked to her, holding her gaze as he approached. There was no fear, only anxiety. He caught her chin between his fingers. "Don't ever beg for anything, Virginia. It doesn't sit well on your shoulders."

"Damn you!" She reached out one small fist and thumped his thigh. "This isn't a joke."

Her eyes plainly showed every emotion she felt. He shut his heart against her turmoil. "I'm sorry. But Kelsey is pregnant, with Wade's baby. Do you know, he wasn't as worried about going to jail as he was concerned with leaving Kelsey alone as a single mother. Wade is determined to take his responsibilities seriously."

Tension vibrated through her body. She bunched the quilt in her lap and held it tight. "If that was so, he wouldn't have gotten her pregnant in the first place."

Dillon lifted his brows. "I suppose that's true enough. But it's spilled milk now. Or rather, spilled—"

"Don't say it!"

He couldn't help it. He chuckled. "You know, Wade didn't exactly act alone. They both played and they both got caught."

"There are alternatives to marriage."

He didn't want to hear her make any suggestions, didn't want her to consider giving the baby away or disposing of it. Narrowing his eyes, he tried to deny the tightening of his gut. "Such as?"

"I could help Kelsey raise it. Women these days don't need a man around to take care of things. Single mothers survive every day. And I could more than provide for them both. She's my sister. The baby would be my niece or nephew."

He relaxed, enough to be distracted by her incredible hair again. He ran his fingertips down a long red curl that reflected the firelight with hints of gold. His fascination with her hair didn't seem to be dwindling as he got used to looking at it. Just the opposite.

And this time Virginia didn't move away. "You're saying Wade would be denied his child? Is that your ingenious plan, Virginia?"

"No... I don't know. I need time to think about it."

"There is no time. Decisions have to be made now. Wade and Kelsey *will* marry. Wade being a member of the family ought to protect him from Cliff in the future. It wouldn't do to have one's brother-in-law in prison, now would it?"

"How do you know Wade didn't do it?" Virginia licked her lips and refused to meet his gaze. "From what I remember, there was pretty strong evidence against him."

His fingers trailed over the curl, then tucked it behind her ear before tilting up her chin. "Do you know what the evidence is?"

A mulish expression came over her face. "You think I'd tell you? In case you're missing something, you're the bad guy in this scenario. I'm the victim. I certainly can't make it easy for you."

He grinned, thinking just how *hard* she made things. "No, I don't suppose you can. Fair enough. You don't give me any details, and I won't give you any more."

Slowly, her brows drew down in a suspicious frown. "Now, wait a minute. That's not fair. I need to know what's going on."

"You need to know only what I tell you."

"That is *not* acceptable!"

"We're not at the office, Virginia. You can't give me orders, because I won't obey them. I don't work for you," he enunciated clearly. "From here on, I'm the one in charge. I know it'll be a new experience for you, but you might as well get used to it."

She practically hummed with anger. "If that's the way you want it, *fine*. But don't expect me to miss the next time I come at you with a frying pan!"

He sat on the edge of the cot. Virginia held the quilt up to cover her breasts, and her rich titian hair hung almost to her elbows. She shook it back. This time, she didn't cower from him when he leaned close, caging her in. Instead, she squared her shoulders and thrust her chin toward him in a silent challenge.

She looked so enticing, which shouldn't have mattered. And it didn't, not in the big picture. But here, closed into the cabin with her, he could feel her presence, could smell the light womanly fragrance of her. He loved how women smelled, and Virginia seemed especially inviting. He braced one hand on the bed beside her hip and used the other to cup her chin, making certain he had her mutinous attention.

"So you deliberately missed the first time, but

you won't be so considerate again? I appreciate the warning, sweetheart. Now I can take necessary precautions."

"What...what do you mean?" Some of her defiance faltered.

"Did you notice that this is the only bed in the room, Virginia?"

Her lips parted and she surveyed the bed as if seeing it for the first time. "It isn't exactly a bed," she sputtered. "It's a narrow little cot that's barely big enough for a single body."

"Then I suppose we'll have to scrunch up real close, won't we? Maybe lay spoon fashion."

She shook her head while color rushed into her cheeks. "You are not getting into this bed with me, Dillon, so forget it."

He grinned, but decided to let her statement pass. "Since you were generous enough to warn me of your intent to lay me low, I guess I should warn you, too. Tonight, I'm going to have to tie you up."

"No!"

"I'd like to wake in the morning with my brains intact. That means," he said, flicking the end of her nose, "I have to restrain you and your more violent tendencies."

"Dillon..."

"Why don't you rest for now, honey? We'll have lunch in a couple of hours."

He walked back into the kitchen, grinning, knowing he'd just set himself up. Virginia would go out of her way to keep from being tied up. But he could handle her. And he'd rather deal with her anger any day than her hurt or fear. Even now, she was probably planning his demise.

He only wished he weren't looking forward to her efforts.

8

HE WAS A GOOD COOK—she'd give him that. But with him watching every bite she took, she felt obliged to skimp. She knew she was overweight, and she didn't want him thinking of her as a glutton. Vanity had no place on a victim's shoulders, but then, she refused to think of herself as a victim. Somehow she'd find a way out of this mess. This wasn't the time to deal with her insecurity about her figure. Besides, she'd already spent years trying.

"Is that all you're going to eat?"

He'd been quiet for so long and her thoughts had been so personal Virginia gave a guilty start. She had to make a grab for the quilt as it started to slide down her body. Dillon watched the path it took and the way she then clutched at it. His gaze locked with hers and remained there.

Awkwardly, she tucked and tugged until the quilt shielded as much of her body as possible. She knew she looked ridiculous with the thing wrapped around her like a sarong, but Dillon flatly refused to return her clothes to her, and she refused to continue cowering in the bed. It was a clash of wills that she fully expected to win. "I, ah, I'm not that hungry."

He made a small sound—a male snort of acknowledgment, then looked away. "You need to eat to keep up your strength. You can't very well give me hell if you're lying in bed too weak to argue, now can you? And I know you haven't eaten all day, so you have to be starved. Come on, finish up."

"No, thank you."

Her stomach muscles tightened, then fluttered, at the searing look he sent her way. "I never thought of you as the fainthearted type, willing to wilt away like a martyr. I thought you were made of sterner stuff." Soft sandy brown hair fell over his brow as he shook his head in mock regret. "You've disappointed me, Virginia."

She thinned her mouth and glared at him. "I have to watch my weight."

Speaking around a large spoonful of meat-filled soup, Dillon asked, "Why?"

He looked genuinely puzzled and she wanted to hit him right between his gorgeous eyes. But he wasn't obtuse, and she assumed he was toying with her. Automatically, her chin lifted. "Because I'm ten pounds overweight, that's why."

"More like twenty." Again, his gaze slid over her, and she felt the touch of it everywhere. "But it looks good on you. Damn good. Makes you nice and round. Skinny women are too pointy. Pointy bones, pointy breasts, pointy hips. Most men prefer a woman with a little meat on her." His gaze lingered on her breasts and her nipples pulled tight in reaction. "Provides a nice cushion."

In her entire life, Virginia had never heard anything so crudely put, or so ridiculous. How

dare he speak to her that way, correcting, insulting and complimenting all in the same breath!
Flustered and confused, she went for a show of
umbrage. "Well, thank you, Mr. Dillon Oaks, for
your masculine insight, but..."

He laughed. "Dillon Oaks *Jr.* to be exact. I
carry my father's name."

Halted in midtirade, she stared at him.
"You're a junior?"

Dillon finished his soup and then carried his
bowl to the sink. "That's right, though I don't
share that fact with just anyone. My father is
rather...infamous in this country. If the connec-
tion was ever made, it could lead to a lot of questions I don't usually want to answer."

Virginia couldn't begin to fathom a Dillon
Oaks Sr. One man of Dillon's caliber, of his ap-
peal and arrogance, was more than the female
populace should have to contend with. "Don't
tell me your father is a kidnapper, also?"

Dillon glanced at her over his hard shoulder,
then began running water in the sink to clean the
dishes. Virginia thought he seemed to be much
more domestically inclined than she was.

"Eat the rest of your soup and I'll tell you."

Obligingly, she ate. What the hell—she was
hungry, and as Dillon had pointed out, he already knew she was overweight, although he
didn't seem to mind. Starving herself for spite
didn't make a bit of sense. Plus he was a wonderful cook. All he'd done was add canned vegeta-
bles and a few spices to meat, but it tasted better
than good. Virginia always ate more when she

was excited or upset; right now, she felt equal parts of both.

Nodding in satisfaction as Virginia dipped her spoon into the bowl, Dillon launched into his first story.

"My father was close to forty and set in his ways when I was born. The military had become his life, and my mother pretty much took him by surprise when she caught him in the States on leave and dumped his newborn infant in his lap. He says it was the biggest shock of his life." Dillon grinned, twin dimples flashing in his darkly tanned cheeks.

"My mother made it clear she didn't want any part of me, and Dad said he could tell by looking at me that I was his kid. Even as a newborn, I had the same dark eyes and light brown hair, and our features are the same, even to this day. Looking at Dad is like looking forty years into the future."

Virginia tried to imagine Dillon as an older, less powerful man, but she couldn't manage it. Somehow she thought Dillon would have a raw strength about him regardless of what exalted age he reached.

He chuckled now, a low rich sound that danced down her spine and sank into her bones. "When my mother started to hand me to Dad, I spit up on her. That was exactly what he wanted to do, but rudeness to a lady went against his grain. Since I'd done it for him, he gladly accepted me. Gradually, he left the military to take on the dubious role of parent."

The image of a man just like Dillon caring for

an infant squeezed something in Virginia's heart, leaving her breathless and captivated.

Dillon tidied the kitchen efficiently, cleaning off the stove and scrubbing the pans. He didn't look as if he needed, wanted or expected her help, which was just as well, because she would have refused. The kidnappee did not help the kidnapper tidy his prison.

Dillon glanced at her, a half smile still hovering around his mouth. "Now, leaving the military might not sound like much to you, but you have to realize my father was an old war dog. He was in active duty in World War II, the Korean War, even the early stages of Vietnam. He had the military haircut, the tattoos and the salty language testifying to his past. He had no idea how to be a civilian, but he did know that without a wife, he couldn't very well raise a child and stay in the army."

Pulling her legs up onto the chair and bracing her heels on the edge, Virginia settled herself more comfortably. She made sure the quilt covered all her vital parts, then wrapped her arms around her knees. The cabin was now cozy and warm, except for the cold air drifting over the hard floor. She leaned her chin on her knees and regarded him. "Did your father ever consider putting you up for adoption?"

He made a rude grunting sound of disbelief. "Not my dad. He admits he didn't know much about parenting, and there were some real rough times, but he'd always believed in taking care of his own. Blood is blood. And you never, for any reason, turn your back on family."

Virginia supposed that accounted for Dillon going to such lengths to rescue Wade. Not that she forgave him just because he had a reason. "So what did your father do then?"

Dillon shrugged. "He tried off and on through the years to get a regular job. But Dad is the original renegade. Ordinary life doesn't suit him. He's not...domestic enough. He doesn't fit in with society, and society is scared to death of him. There's a rough, almost dangerous edge to him that people pick up on within seconds of meeting him." He sent her a mischievous grin. "It scares the hell out of most men, and excites most women."

It sounded as if there was a lot of his father in Dillon, she thought, letting her gaze stray over his hard body, taking in the broad muscled back, the tattered jeans over solid thighs and tight, narrow hips. He had a natural arrogance that set him apart from other men, a self-confidence that went beyond being big and handsome and capable.

There was an aura of danger about him—something about the intensity of his eyes—that was very appealing. She could easily believe he shared that trait with his father. Curiosity got the better of her and she asked quietly, "Were you ever afraid of him?"

Dillon turned to face her, leaning back on the counter and crossing his arms over his broad chest. "No. I was afraid for him a lot, though. There were times when he'd be out of the country for long stretches—a month or more. I'd get antsy and nervous, but he always came back."

"Who watched you then? Who raised you?"

Dillon chewed the side of his mouth, his gaze on a far wall. "Dad always had one woman or another hanging around. They swarmed to him. When he had to leave, he'd give one of them money to make certain I made it to school and ate regular."

Virginia couldn't imagine such an existence. Knowing her words to be cruel, but unable to help herself, she said, "Maybe you would have been better off adopted. At least you would have had a parent who spent time with you!"

He gave her a pitying look and shook his head. "Dad spent more time with me than most kids ever hope to get. He taught me everything he knew—how to protect myself, how to get what I need, how to stay ahead and take care of those people who depend on me. He taught me morals and values and personal ethics and self-worth." His gaze was hard, almost accusing. "He taught me about the world."

She shouldn't ask. Knowing about Dillon's life and his family would only get her more involved. But the words couldn't be held back. She *wanted* to know everything about him, even more than she wanted to be free. "If he was such a great father, why did he leave you?"

When Dillon turned back to the dishes, Virginia wondered if she'd pushed too far, if maybe he wouldn't answer her at all. Then his voice, soft and low, came to her. "Dad became a mercenary. He continued to do the things he knew how to do best, but he did them on his own time...and for a lot more money."

For some reason, she wanted to go to him, to hold him. She shook her head. Touching him would be a very dangerous thing. To her heart.

"Your father was a hired killer?"

"You make him sound like an assassin." He cast her a glance. "He didn't exactly run around slitting innocent throats. His job was generally to apprehend and hold. And more often than not, it was the government who hired him for assignments they couldn't get sanctioned through the regular channels. Not always, though. He worked for other agencies, too. And he came through for them every time."

"You sound proud." If her parents had taken part in illegal activities, she would have died from shame. But Dillon actually seemed pleased by his father's sordid accomplishments.

He flattened his palms on the edge of the sink and looked out the window. "I don't know that 'proud' is the right word. But I know my dad did whatever had to be done so he could keep me. He made certain I understood how much he cared about me, that I was the first priority in his life. I've always known that no matter what, he's there for me. It doesn't matter if I'm right or wrong, if I'm in danger, he'll back me up." Dillon was silent a moment, then added, "That's what family's about. Unqualified support."

She'd never thought about her family in those particular terms. Sure her parents had loved her, even though she hadn't been their favorite. But Dillon spoke as if life was a war, filled with risks and hazards and deviousness. She supposed, given his upbringing, that might have been the only world he'd known.

She felt that tightening in her chest again and had to take several breaths. She would *not* feel sorry for him. What he'd done was unforgivable. She didn't for a minute believe that nonsense about taking her to protect her. He planned to ransack her office and defend his brother. If Cliff caught him at it, Dillon would go to jail. She had to find a way to reason with him. He had to let her go.

Dillon carried a dishrag to the table and began to wipe the surface. "I'm proficient with every weapon there is, but I'm especially good with my hands. Dad started teaching me self-defense when I was about six, after he got home from a mission to find out his girlfriend had taken off and left me alone. He wanted to be sure that if it ever happened again, I'd know how to take care of myself. He taught me all about security, how to create it, how to break it." He grinned. "That information is what got me hired by your company."

Hesitating for only a second, she asked, "Have you followed in your father's footsteps? Do you hire yourself out as a mercenary?"

"No." His black eyes flashed, and he smiled. "Kidnapping you is the only time I've walked on the wrong side of the law. I own a horse ranch, and Dad lives with me now. For the most part, that keeps me plenty busy enough. Over the years, before Dad mellowed and settled down, I bailed him out of a few situations that hadn't gone quite as planned. And I went with him on a few jobs. But they were legit, and I learned a lot. And I have to admit, my skills have come in handy recently."

Virginia sighed theatrically. "Wonderful. I get to be your guinea pig?"

He leaned his hip against the table and considered her. "Yeah. But I swear I think storming an enemy platoon would have been easier than taking you." He touched the swollen bruise on the bridge of his nose. "Do you plan to keep abusing me?"

"Not if you plan to turn me loose anytime soon," she replied sweetly.

Dillon chuckled again. His mood seemed to have improved quite a bit. In fact, she couldn't remember him ever being so relaxed. She wasn't sure she liked it; it made him appear less dangerous—and more appealing than ever.

As if he'd read her thoughts, he laughed and then tapped her chin. "Want to play cards?"

The quick switch threw her and she stared at him. "You're kidding, right?"

"We're stuck here for a while, Virginia. There's no television, certainly no outdoor activities. I can see that active mind of yours churning, but I won't be letting you go, so relax. Why make us both miserable?"

"Because you deserve to be miserable?"

"But you don't. So why not loosen up. We still have a few hours before bedtime."

Thinking of bedtime made her shiver and she looked away; beneath the quilt, her body turned warm, too warm. Nothing in her life had prepared her for this man. She had no idea how to deal with him. At the moment, sarcasm seemed her only option, the only way to keep the distance between them. "Do you plan to leave me here alone while you ransack my office?"

"Yes, tomorrow morning. But you don't need to worry. You'll be safe enough."

"Safe? What if something happens? I mean, there's no phone anywhere around here for me to call for help. And I assume we have no close neighbors."

He went to a cabinet and pulled out a battered deck of cards. "No. There's no phone nearby, no one to hear you scream. When I leave to check things out, you'll be on your own. But as you keep telling me, you can take care of yourself. It'll only be a few hours."

She struggled not to reveal her reaction to his words. If he left her alone, she'd finally have a chance to escape. Surely the truck would leave tracks, and she could follow them to the main road. There would have to be traffic of some kind, and she'd hitch a ride—

Damn, she needed her clothes! She couldn't very well go outside in what she wore now. Not only would she freeze, but no one would pick her up. They'd all think she was a lunatic.

Realizing that, she glared at Dillon. "I'm cold. Why don't you at least give me back my sweater." She'd work on the other clothes as she went along, slowly earning his trust and gaining back her whole outfit, especially her boots. They weren't exactly designed for treks in this kind of weather, but they'd have to suffice.

Dillon laid out a game of solitaire. Without

looking at her, he said, "You're not an idiot, Virginia. You should know better than to underestimate me." He glanced up, and there was regret in his eyes, but determination, as well. "There is absolutely no way for you to leave this cabin. We're miles from everything, and the snow is piling up. By morning, it'll be a couple of feet deep."

She lifted her chin. "You plan to leave."

"The truck is four-wheel drive. You're not. If you tried to leave here by foot, you'd freeze to death—even with your clothes. If you're not worried about your own hide, think of the company. Under Cliff's sole guidance, it wouldn't last long. We both know it."

Frustration nearly smothered her. "Bastard."

He seemed unruffled by her insult. "I can make you a deal, you know."

Oh, the way he said that, with his voice husky and low and suggestive. Her thighs tightened reflexively, and she searched his face for a clue to his mood, but his expression was inscrutable. Cautiously, she asked, "What kind of deal?" Her voice broke, and she had to clear her throat. Even with his head down, she saw Dillon smile.

"Virginia, Virginia," he chided. "What are you thinking? Here I am, offering you a legitimate exchange, but you insist on laying evil deeds at my door."

Her feet hit the floor hard and she put both palms on the table. His teasing made her feel like a fool. "Let's see. Beyond kidnapping, drugging and stealing a woman's clothes, what else might you be capable of? I'd say the possibilities are endless!"

His humor vanished, and his tone turned gentle. "I told you I wouldn't hurt you."

"You also told me you—" Appalled, she stopped herself. Had she really been about to berate him for not wanting her sexually? The truth of that hurt, but damned if she wanted to let him know it. She crossed her arms tightly over her chest and slouched back in her chair.

A strained silence fell between them. She could feel his gaze, but she refused to meet it. Instead, she stared at the fireplace until her vision blurred and she could breathe normally again.

Somehow Dillon seemed to know the moment she regained control. He returned his attention to his cards as if nothing had happened. "You give me the evidence Cliff has on Wade, give me a chance to prove it's false, and I'll take you back that much sooner. Maybe you could even help me figure out who the embezzler is. I know you're a woman who likes control, who needs to be kept informed. You might enjoy the challenge."

He never looked at her, just continued to play the game, moving and adjusting the cards at his leisure. His attitude infuriated her, but she didn't think she could stand not knowing. Her pride had forbade her to ask again, but now he had offered.

And what would it matter if he knew the evidence? If anything, it might convince him to get his brother out of the country, instead of involving Kelsey in his ridiculous scheme. One thing was certain, though. Never would she tell him it was she who had found the evidence of missing funds, not Cliff. Dillon's reaction to that news wasn't something she wanted to experience while she remained his captive.

She drew a deep breath, considering. Dillon laid the ace of spades at the top of his line of cards.

"Will it make things easier on you if I tell you what evidence Cliff has?"

"It might hurry things along a little. But the outcome will be the same either way." Now he did look up, and the hardness in his expression chilled her. She shivered and wrapped her arms around her knees.

"Regardless of what you do or don't tell me, I'm not letting my brother go to jail to satisfy Cliff's warped sense of obligation to his sister."

Virginia couldn't look away. "That's what you think all this is about? You think Cliff got upset because Kelsey was seeing your brother, so he concocted this whole scheme just to get Wade out of the picture?"

"That's how a coward fights. Backhanded, through lies and deception."

"Coming from you, that doesn't say much!"

"I give as good as I get." He flipped another card. "Kelsey knew how Cliff would react. It's my opinion that's why she started chasing Wade in the first place. At the time, he was involved with Laura Neil and wouldn't even have noticed Kelsey. But she knew you two would have a conniption if she got involved with the hired help."

"But we didn't know!"

"Cliff found out. And not long after that, he decided Wade had been embezzling."

God, had she inadvertently handed Cliff the perfect tool for revenge? When she'd given him the faulty accounts, she'd known immediately that his satisfaction, in balance with his rage, had been too keen. At the time, she hadn't suspected anyone, she'd only wanted the matter looked into. She was even running her own private investigation. But Cliff had jumped on it, and it hadn't taken him long at all to blame Wade Sanders.

She leaned forward and rested her elbows on the table, but that drew Dillon's gaze to her breasts, and she quickly sat back again. Frowning, she tried to understand his reasoning, to sort it all out in her mind. Blaming Wade may have been convenient, knowing how Cliff felt about Kelsey. He considered her his only ally, his family, in a way Virginia had ceased to be soon after their parents' deaths. Cliff wasn't beyond doing something so reprehensible if it suited his purposes. She just didn't think he was quick-witted enough to concoct such a scheme.

There were also a lot of facts to deal with, beyond the emotional issues. Virginia felt as if too much was hitting her a one time. She couldn't quite sort it all out. "You're telling me Cliff's known for some time that Kelsey and your brother were seeing each other, but he never mentioned it to me?"

"I think he expected to take care of it on his own, without your interference." He flipped over another card, only briefly scanning the deck

before returning his gaze to her face. "You treat
Cliff like a little boy. It's no wonder he sneaks
around trying to do something, anything, on his
own."

"You're defending him!"

"Don't get me wrong. I think he's a fool—" his
gaze narrowed on her face "—for letting you dictate to him. A real man would have taken charge
long ago."

Virginia forgot her precarious position as victim; she forgot that she needed to trade information and sort out facts. She forgot everything except her pride. Running the company was all she
had, the only truly wonderful thing she'd ever
accomplished. It defined her life, her integrity,
her strength, her independence. And now Dillon
would strip that from her with a few callous
words. She'd worked hard to get that modicum
of business respect; she wouldn't let him or anyone else take it from her.

She came to her feet so fast her chair tipped
over, landing with a crash in the silent cabin. She
whirled to storm away, only to come up short
when Dillon grabbed the back of the quilt. Like a
dog running out of leash, she jerked to a stop.
Staring straight ahead, she saw nothing but the
walls, a tiny enclosure with no place to go, no
place to run. She nearly choked on her bitterness,
and then Dillon began tugging on the quilt, reel-
ing her in.

She would have released it, but then he had
her arm in an unbreakable grip, and it took only
one small yank for her to fall solidly into his lap.
Without any real effort on his part, he subdued

her struggles. To her mortification, tears threatened. She'd never felt so vulnerable or helpless. Or hurt. She didn't like it. Lifting one fist, she thudded it against his shoulder, which felt like hitting a boulder.

Dillon didn't so much as flinch. "Don't you want to know how I would have taken control, Virginia?"

She shook her head, or at least she tried. Dillon had curled her so close her cheek pressed into the solid wall of his chest. Beyond all her anger and frustration, she felt an awareness of him, of the hardness of his body, his incredible scent, the gentleness of his hands as one coasted over her back and the other tangled in her hair. Effortlessly, he had surrounded and invaded her.

"I'm going to tell you anyway."

She felt the light touch of his mouth against her hair, and everything inside her seemed to shift and swell. Her body pulsed with awareness. She didn't know what that small kiss meant, or what she should do about it.

"Virginia, I would have made you a visible partner. I would have used your obvious strengths for the benefit of the company. Anyone who meets you knows you have an air of command, that you can aptly take charge of any situation. Cliff's biggest mistake is in trying to steal from you what you do best, instead of using it to his and the company's advantage. By giving you the credit you deserve, he would have gained a portion of that control."

The praise stunned her. Carefully, she tipped her head back to see his face. His mouth was only a few inches from her own, his expression implacable and hard. At the moment, there seemed to be no tenderness about him, but she knew better. "You're only trying to soften me up."

"No, baby. You're soft enough as it is."

Her eyes narrowed, but before she could speak, his fingers tightened in her hair like a rough caress and he kissed her temple. "You know what I say is true, Virginia. Cliff could only make himself look better with you at his side. He's a fool for keeping you in the shadows."

"So I've told him."

Dillon grinned and those dimples, so seldom seen, charmed her, adding to the heat that kept gathering beneath her skin, weakening her muscles. "I know you have. Repeatedly and with a great deal of vehemence. It's the way you tell him that makes him dig in his heels. You need to learn a little about compromise."

Virginia couldn't help but grin, too. "Lectured by a kidnapper. What's the world coming to?"

Dillon cupped her head, his fingers thrusting deep into her hair. "Tell me what evidence he has, Virginia."

She sighed. There was really no harm in telling him, even if his motives hadn't been firmly established. And for some reason, she felt more generous now than she had a few minutes ago. "All right."

She straightened, prepared to leave the warmth and comfort of Dillon's lap, but his hands tightened and she knew she couldn't move unless he let her. It didn't seem worth the struggle, so she relented. She really didn't want to move anyway.

She had to pick her words carefully, to give him only the bare bones of it, leaving out her own involvement. "As you probably already know, Wade Sanders was fired. I wanted to give him an indefinite leave of absence, but Cliff wouldn't hear of it. I believe he gave Sanders some vague excuse about too many errors at first, not wanting to tip anyone off." That had actually been her suggestion, the only one Cliff had listened to. Though Cliff had been adamant about firing Wade, Virginia hadn't wanted to take the chance that they might fire the wrong man. Wade had been with them for several years and never caused any problems.

Why wouldn't Cliff listen to her? Now look at the trouble they were in.

Of course, she hadn't known Kelsey was seeing Wade. Which wasn't surprising. Other than organizing the donations made by the company to various charities, Kelsey never involved herself in business. She and Kelsey and Cliff all led separate lives, with different priorities. Virginia made the business her life, while Kelsey chose to keep herself apart, both emotionally and physically. Lately, the two sisters seldom talked.

The gentle movement of Dillon's fingers on her scalp lulled her, and she went on with a sigh. "It was all done quietly, with no suspicions being announced. That way, if Wade wasn't the one embezzling the funds, the embezzlement would have continued and they could have trapped the person responsible. But since Wade was fired, no more money has been taken."

She looked at Dillon, at the concentrated frown on his brow, the dark eyes intense with thought. She wanted to soothe him, to comfort him, because in her heart she believed his brother to be guilty. And she knew it was going to come as a terrible blow to him.

He had some antiquated notion of family honor that wouldn't allow him to believe his brother capable of embezzlement. The contradictions in him amazed and intrigued her. He was by far the most dangerous man she'd ever met, but at the moment, bizarre as it seemed, she trusted him implicitly. The same code that would force him to risk his own life for his brother would keep him from ever deliberately hurting her. When he said he only wanted to save his brother, she believed him.

"Dillon, since the day Wade was relieved of his position, no more money has been taken," she repeated. "The investigation has been very quiet. Other than the two professionals Cliff hired to find proof that it was embezzlement and not accounting errors, no one knew except Cliff, Wade and me."

Idly, Dillon traced his fingers up and down her bare arm while he stared toward the fire. His light brown hair shone with highlights from the flames and his dark, dark eyes seemed almost fathomless. More contrasts, Virginia thought, and not only his coloring. He seemed contemplative and regretful, but beneath it all, the internal conviction of his brother's innocence was still there.

"Dillon? Don't you see? No one else knew except Wade. Not knowing the theft had been discovered, the embezzler probably would have continued to steal. But it didn't happen. The fact that the embezzlement ended the day Wade left the company almost proves his guilt." Almost, though Virginia wanted solid proof, and that's why she'd set up her own investigation.

Dillon finally looked at her. His large rough hand rose to cup her cheek, his thumb stroking over her temple. Slowly, inexhoribly, he urged her closer, and his mouth began to lower.

Virginia didn't know what to think, what to do. A whispering roared in her ears, and she accepted the fact that she wanted his kiss more than was wise. Pride, determination, common sense, seemed to evaporate. All she could concentrate on was the scent of Dillon, the hard comfort of his body, the way her own body reacted to him.

When his mouth touched hers, without passion but with tenderness and concern, she wanted to snuggle closer and stay safe, with him, in this cabin.

The thought appalled her, but before she could pull away, he lifted his head and then set her on her feet. "It's almost bedtime, honey. Why don't you go take a shower or do whatever it is women do to get ready for bed."

Stupified, Virginia stared down at him. She swayed before catching herself and locking her knees against the weakness he caused. "Didn't you hear what I said? Didn't you understand? Wade is guilty."

Dillon gathered up the cards and stacked them neatly in his palm. "Go on, Virginia. There are clean towels in the bathroom, and I unpacked your shampoo and cleanser and all that other feminine stuff you had in that tiny bag."

He stood and Virginia reached out to clutch at his shirt. Dillon stared down at her, his expression veiled. She wanted to shake him, to make him understand that this would never work, that he was trying to save his brother against all odds.

"Dillon, you can't go through with this! You'll only implicate yourself in Wade's actions."

He pried her fingers loose from his shirt and then held her hand close to his chest. "You're wrong, honey. You say Wade is the only one who knew, but don't you wonder how I knew it was embezzlement he was suspected of, before any charges could be made? Don't you wonder how Wade contacted me so quickly that I was able to set this whole damn thing up *before* Cliff even began his investigation?"

"I...I hadn't really thought about it." She felt a stirring of dread, of sick premonition.

Dillon turned her toward the bathroom and gave her a light push. "It's easy, Virginia. Someone else knew. If Cliff didn't make it up or take the money himself, and if there really is money missing and Wade doesn't have it, someone else is guilty. Maybe the same person who's trying to hurt you. Maybe even the person who warned Wade in the first place."

"Why would anyone do that?"

"For the same reason you tried to keep it quiet. If the embezzlement stopped, Wade would look guilty. And who could look more innocent than the person trying to save him?"

She held on to the bathroom doorknob and looked back at Dillon. She felt both hope and dread that it might be all over. "If Wade didn't do it and you think you know who did, then the problem is solved. We can forget this little charade and go home. I promise you I'll do all I can to settle this."

But Dillon shook his head. "Are you forgetting the threats against you? And don't shake your pretty head at me, damn it. Someone cut your brake lines. And someone came into your house, using a key. If I hadn't been with you, I don't know what might have happened. But I do know I don't like the idea of anyone hurting you. I won't let it happen."

He took a step toward her, before stopping himself. "I'm sorry, Virginia. But the *problem* is far from solved. In fact, things just got a whole hell of a lot more complicated. Because I happen to think the two problems are related. And that narrows our suspect list down considerably.

9

SHE WANTED HIM to explain, but Dillon couldn't find the heart to tell her the truth. Not yet. Not until he had more information. Explaining to Wade was going to be tough enough, something he already dreaded.

He'd gotten used to the idea of blaming Cliff, and it felt good to blame him. But Cliff couldn't have been working alone because he wasn't savvy enough to pull off such a stunt. He should have realized that sooner.

Dillon believed the embezzlement charge and the threat to Virginia were related. That meant Cliff was the one tampering with her car and hiding out in her house or he'd hired someone else to do it. Either way, Dillon intended to destroy them all. He only hoped Virginia wouldn't be destroyed in the process.

Facing the fireplace, he listened to the sound of the shower and knew Virginia was only yards away, naked and wet and worried. Lord, he wanted her, wanted to hold her and comfort her and protect her from her damn deranged family and their deadly manipulations. Kissing her earlier had been so sweet, an odd feeling he'd never experienced before. There had been no passion, at least not on the surface where she would detect it. He'd simply been holding her on his lap, aware of her turmoil, sensing her insecurity. And he'd kissed her as a sign of comfort and understanding.

It was the first time he could recall sharing such a thing with a woman. Usually, if he kissed a woman, it was a foregone conclusion that they'd end up in bed. He didn't have the time or the interest for romantic relationships, so he settled for sexual ones. He'd always been discreet, and very careful with his health and the issue of responsibility, but he'd never claimed to be a monk. He enjoyed women, and in return he made sure they enjoyed him.

Yet he'd kissed Virginia, knowing he couldn't make love to her, knowing she was the one woman off-limits to him. And it had been so incredibly tender he'd wanted to go on holding and kissing her all night.

Of course, that hadn't been the only feeling storming him at that moment. Having her on his lap caused his body to surge in awareness. The firm pressure of her behind had been incredibly arousing and had stirred up visions of how they could mate, leaving his brain muddled with erotic images of her naked and warm and wet.

Not only did he want to comfort and gentle her, he wanted to claim her, to make love to her while she sat on his lap in just that way, her breasts vulnerable to his hands and mouth, her legs draped over his flanks. He wanted to break down her rigid defenses and force her to be a woman, his woman. He wanted to hear her whisper his name while he manipulated her to a blinding climax again and again. He would bury himself so deep inside her lush body she'd forget everything and everyone else. But that was impossible, as well as unconscionable. He wouldn't take advantage of her, no matter how severe his own need became.

So he'd settled for that one chaste kiss of comfort, and strangely, he'd reveled in it.

The shower finally shut off and Dillon closed his eyes, imagining her drying her body, the soft towel moving over her generous curves, around her full breasts, between her plump thighs.... His erection was almost painful, but he couldn't control the reaction of his body. He stood, then paced to the window over the sink. The snow fell continuously, burying everything, serving his purpose nicely. The deeper it got, the less he had to worry about Virginia trying to run off when he left her in the morning. Travel would be difficult enough for him, even with the truck. He'd have to adjust his time frame to accommodate the extra hours it would take to maneuver the icy roads.

The bathroom door opened and he turned to see Virginia peeking out.

"I need something clean to put on."

He sighed, ruthlessly bringing himself back under control. "We've been over this already, Virginia. I'm not taking any chances, which means the less you wear, the safer you'll be."

Her lips firmed and her slim auburn brows drew down in a frown. The severe look was a familiar one to him, but mixed with the incongruity of her cowering body behind the door, it almost made him smile.

"Fine. I understand that. But don't expect me to put on the same thing I've been wearing all day. Give me something else."

He considered that for a moment, then nodded. "I'll be right back."

As he headed for the door, she said, "Dillon!" and he heard the alarm. It made his insides twist with regret, because he was solely responsible for making her so uncertain, for stealing away her cockiness and arrogance. "I'm not leaving, honey. I'm just going out to the truck to fetch one of my shirts."

He saw every thought that flashed through her quick mind, and he laughed. "Don't get any ideas about bashing me over the head and stealing my clothes or my truck. I've disconnected a few things on the engine, and it won't run again until I reconnect them—easy enough for me, but unless you know a lot about mechanics, you won't get the thing started. And my suitcase only has a few shirts and clean skivvies anyway. Except for trying to strip my jeans off me, you'd have to leave here bare assed."

Her response was to slam the bathroom door in his face.

As Dillon dashed through the snow to the truck, he realized he wore a sappy grin on his face. Damn, but the woman amused him with her flash temper and biting wit. Now that he was no longer constrained to keep his natural responses to himself, he actually enjoyed her sharp tongue. They played a game of dominance, and even though he knew he'd come out ahead, that in the end he could conquer her if that was his wish, the game still thrilled him. Virginia proved a worthy adversary and she kept him on his toes.

When he returned to the cabin with a spare white T-shirt for her and a few things for himself, he did so cautiously. He didn't doubt her ability to take him by surprise; she'd already done so numerous times. But Virginia was still in the bathroom, and when he knocked, she merely stuck her hand out through the narrowly opened door.

After she'd snatched the shirt from him, he heard a muttered, "Thank you." He went back to sitting by the fire.

He didn't know quite how to handle her now, but he had decided to give her options. He'd found in the past that it was easier for people to accept the idea of having choices than being totally dominated. Not that he was looking forward to his next move. Hell, it would likely be much harder on him than it would be on her. At the moment, she pretty much detested him—rightfully so—while his feelings came nowhere close to such a negative emotion. But he didn't want her fighting him, either, and possibly hurting herself. He had to find a way to gain her compliance so she could get some badly needed sleep and he could relax his guard.

Turning as the bathroom door opened again, he watched Virginia creep across the floor with the quilt thrown over her shoulders and held close to her breasts by a tight fist. It dragged be-

hind her like a queen's robe and suited her
haughty stature better than she could know.

She wore his shirt. He could see the hem of the
white T-shirt brushing her dimpled knees as she
walked, and the sight filled him with a primitive
satisfaction. The shirt signified a claim, a stake he
couldn't make but wanted all the same.

Ignoring her wary gaze, Dillon came to his feet
and braced himself for the newest confrontation.
"Into the bed, Virginia."

She faltered and her beautiful eyes widened,
looking more amber than gold in the dim room.
They seemed to dominate her face, a face
scrubbed clean of makeup, pink and fresh and
young. He knew she was thirty years old, but at
the moment, she barely looked nineteen. As
usual, her chin went into the air and her shoulders squared.

"What are you going to do?"

He picked up the rope he'd laid on the mantel.
Gently, he said, "I told you I'd have to tie you, remember?"

"No!"

"I can't take a chance on you doing anything
foolish."

"You're not going to tie me, Dillon."

The warning was there, but the trembling in
her tone belied the vehemence of her words. He
felt like an animal, and he hated himself, hated
what he had to do. He clenched his hands into
fists, tightened his abdomen and said, "There's
only one other choice."

Hope shone in her eyes, mixed with the caution she tried so hard to hide. "What choice?"

"I'll have to sleep with you." She took a quick step back, and he said, "It's one way or the other, Virginia. I'm a light sleeper, and if I'm right beside you, I'll know if you try anything. But if you hate the thought of having me so close, I can sleep in a chair. It wouldn't be the first time." He stared at her, refusing to back down from the accusation on her face, refusing to acknowledge the stirring of lust that twisted his gut and tightened his groin. "But then I'll have to tie you. Those are your choices."

"Which leaves me no choice at all."

The rope slid through his fingers as he wound and rewound it. "Don't be bitter, honey. Accept what has to be. We both need some sleep."

With her gaze on the rope, she chewed her lip and squirmed, and it was so unlike her, this indecisiveness, that he almost relented. Hell, he could go another night without sleep. He could easily sit by the fire and watch her all night as she rested; it would be an apt punishment for involving her in all this, for using her.

"All right."

Taken by surprise, Dillon stared at her, wanting no mistakes, no illusions. "All right what?"

"You can sleep with me."

She tried to scoff, shrugging her rounded shoulders and shifting her feet nervously. She wouldn't meet his gaze, no matter how he willed her to.

"I mean, what's the big deal? You've already made it clear you don't want me. Right?"

He didn't—couldn't—answer. Surely the woman wasn't blind to his lust; at thirty years of age she'd had lovers, or so he'd understood. Virginia was in no way a naive spinster who wouldn't recognize the signs.

The material of his worn jeans was straining he was so hard. He felt huge, hot and throbbing, and it wouldn't take much more than a single touch from her to make him come. The thought caused a shudder to skip down his rigid spine. He held his breath in reaction.

Even an inexperienced woman would notice such an obvious arousal. He wasn't a small man, not in any way. But then, Virginia tried not to look at him, and he'd never seen her this distracted, this...*shy*. His heart twisted.

When he remained silent, she went on, determined to brazen it out. "We'll be separated by a quilt and we could use the shared warmth tonight when the fire dies down."

"Fine." Dillon put the rope back up on the mantel and snatched up his own change of clothes as he headed for the bathroom. Right now, he needed a cold shower, and given the size of the hot water tank, that was likely all that was left. "Get into bed. I'll be there in just a few minutes."

He didn't wait to see Virginia's reaction to his curt order. He didn't want to be tempted further by the sight of her, by the length of her gorgeous, sexy hair, her bare feet or wide-eyed gaze.

He didn't want to think about lying close to her warm soft body but not touching her in all the ways that tempted him most.

In the bathroom, he leaned back against the door, then opened his eyes and met the sight of her pale silk teddy draped over the towel bar. She'd rinsed the thing out, but the material was so sheer it already looked dry in places.

Like a sleepwalker, he stepped over and raised it in his hand. Cool, smooth. Damp. He lifted the material to his nose and drank in her woman-soft, musky scent, knowing the delicious smell would be so much stronger on her body, her heated skin. His pulse throbbed and he rubbed the slippery material over his cheek. Finally, disgusted with his self-torture and the expected results, he draped the teddy back on the towel bar and turned on the water.

It took him only minutes to realize the cold shower wasn't cold enough. His skin prickled with the chill, but still he felt hot and aroused, his loins full and heavy, his muscles drawn too tight. He couldn't go to her this way, on the very edge of exploding. Not only would he frighten her, he'd be testing his control beyond dangerous limits. Since no woman had ever had this effect on him, he felt angry and helpless at his inability to deal with it. With a curse, he made up his mind.

The shower was barely wide enough for his shoulders, but he braced his back against the icy tile wall and closed his eyes. The freezing water sprayed his face and chest and groin like sharp needles and he allowed that feeling, allowed it to grow and torment him until he couldn't breathe. Then he relieved the pressure.

It didn't take much, not with the way he'd been aroused all day. When his climax hit, he clenched his teeth and growled, pressing his shoulders hard against the cold wall. The feelings went on and on and finally he slumped on a ragged groan, his body slowly relaxing.

With his lust diminished but far from gone, he left the shower. His thighs still trembled, his breathing still uneven. Shivering, he briskly dried himself, then pulled on his underwear and shoved his legs back into his jeans. Normally, he slept in the nude, but lying beside Virginia without the protection of sturdy denim would be disastrous, even after his release. He wasn't a fool, and he knew his own limitations. After fingercombing his hair and brushing his teeth, he quietly left the bathroom.

The cabin seemed too silent, and he wondered for a brief instant if Virginia would launch another attack; he wasn't at all up to fending her off. But then he saw her in the bed, curled on her side, the quilt tucked tightly around her, her hands beneath her cheek. The fireplace cast a dancing golden glow over everything, but especially on her hair, which fanned out behind her and covered a good portion of the bed, including the part where he would lay.

She kept her eyes tightly closed, even though he knew she wasn't asleep.

Shadows in the darkest parts of the cabin seemed to insulate them from any intrusion. The fire hissed and the air smelled pleasantly of winter and wood smoke and Virginia.

The bed dipped as he put one knee beside her hip. She clutched at the edge of the mattress to keep from rolling toward him. He watched her eyes squeeze a little tighter, her shoulders hunch, and he wanted to yell, to shout out his frustration like a madman. Ill equipped to handle sleeping chastely with a woman who turned him on, he felt angry, at himself and her. He remained poised beside her for several heartbeats while he took deep breaths and resigned himself to the inevitable.

"I'll have to curl around you to fit on the bed."

She didn't respond. Cautiously, he stretched out full length beside her, pulling the spare quilt over his body, then flipping the extra over her so that she was covered by both quilts. The room would get chillier as the night wore on and the fire burned down. Virginia never moved a muscle.

Reaching over, he caught her waist and pulled her snugly against his body. She made a small sound, then went perfectly still again. His body hummed with tension. "Try to relax, honey. I never bite a woman unless she asks me to."

Her elbow came back with surprising force. He grunted even as he grinned, then tightened his arm in a quick hug. "That's better. I thought maybe you were concentrating on playing possum."

"Actually, I was concentrating on pretending you don't exist."

He chuckled at her continued sarcasm, able to see the irony now that she wasn't so frozen beside him. "You know that's not going to work. Not with us both so cozy in this bed." Feeling her bottom tucked snug against his groin worked wonders to revive his libido; his earlier release might never have happened.

"It could work if you'd shut up and let me get to sleep."

He hugged her again, pressing his nose to the back of her neck and breathing in the sweet fragrance of her hair. It felt soft on his face, and he wondered how soft it would feel on the rest of his body. Just as quickly, he chased the stirring thought away, sensing disaster. "Good night, Virginia."

Several minutes passed, and she remained motionless. Dillon thought she had dozed off until she whispered, "Dillon?"

"Hmm?"

Again she was silent, before finally asking, "What would you do if Wade was guilty?"

He nuzzled her ear, unable to help himself, and was rewarded with her slight shiver. He decided masochistic tendencies must be part of his genetic makeup. "First, I suppose I'd beat the hell out of him."

Virginia half turned to see him and they nearly bumped noses. Her face showed astonishment as she searched his gaze for sincerity. "Your own brother?"

Firelight licked over her cheekbones, turning her eyelashes to gold and making her skin glisten. Dillon tucked a loose curl behind her ear, that damn tenderness tightening his chest again, mixing with the lust to confuse and agitate him. "Especially my brother. I couldn't let him go to jail, but I'd definitely want him to understand that what he'd done was wrong, and there's always a price to be paid. We'd eventually talk about it, I suppose, and hopefully I could make him understand so the situation never occurred again."

Virginia considered his words, then turned back to her pillow. "I think it's really nice that you care so much. Not many families are that way."

"What about you, Virginia?" he asked tentatively, trying to find the right words. "What would you do if you found out Cliff or Kelsey had broken the law? What if Cliff resorted to blackmail...or Kelsey put herself at risk for money? What would you do?"

She shook her head. "I don't know. Things aren't as clear-cut for me as they are for you."

"You love your brother and sister."

"Yes. But we don't usually see eye to eye. We don't have the rapport that you evidently have with Wade and your father."

He smoothed his hand up and over her shoulder, then back to her elbow. "You could have, if you'd be willing to work for it." He wanted to stop touching her, but he couldn't seem to help himself and his fingers lingered on her soft white skin.

"It might be too late now. If you get your way, and Kelsey marries Wade, nothing will ever be the same again. Our family will be more divided than ever."

"You can't know that. Problems have a way of either destroying a family or bringing it together. If you'd give Wade half a chance, and trust my judgment just a bit, you might find things are in better shape than ever."

"Ha!" Again she twisted to see him and her

cheeks were flushed with righteous indignation.
"Not only do you kidnap me, but now you refuse
to tell me who you suspect of setting this whole
thing up. How can I possibly trust you?"

"Give me a little time." He splayed his fingers
over her belly and heard her audible gasp. Her
soft stomach quivered before he felt her muscles
tighten. "Give me a chance to check things out, to
get my facts straight, and then I'll tell you what I
know."

"When?"

"Tomorrow when I get back."

"I could leave while you're gone, you know."

"But you won't." Dillon was painfully aware
of their present situation, their lying together in
intimate surroundings, the night dark and the
fire warm, talking in bed like an old married couple. Virginia seemed to have put her uneasiness
aside for the moment. That alone proved some
measure of trust. "You're not afraid of me, for
yourself or your family. There's no reason for
you to run."

"You can't know what I'm feeling!"

"But I do. You trust me not to hurt you. Trust
me enough to find out what I can tomorrow, then
we'll decide together what to do."

She chewed her lip in indecision. "You'll tell
me everything? All your suspicions? Anything
you find out?"

"I promise."

Her sigh was long and dramatic. "It's a sorry
day when I take the word of a kidnapper, but I
suppose I have no choice." She dropped her
head back to her pillow and wiggled to get more

comfortable. It was Dillon's turn to suck in his breath. Virginia seemed to have difficulty getting settled, and finally she punched her pillow. "Cliff is going to give me hell for this whole mess."

Dillon grabbed her hips to still her movements before he forgot his good intentions and shoved her T-shirt high and threw the quilts off the bed. He wanted to feel her bare buttocks moving against him. "I have no doubt you'll give as good as you get. Cliff doesn't stand a chance."

"Good night, Dillon."

He let his body ease against hers, moving his arm around her waist, the other under her pillow, supporting her head. *He* wasn't comfortable; he was too alert for comfort. But he thought he might eventually sleep. Tomorrow would be horrendous, filled with confrontations, and he'd need a little sleep if he was to deal with the difficulties in the best way.

About a half hour later, he heard Virginia's breathing taper into sleep and her body sighed into his, warm and feminine and soft, fitting against him perfectly. He stared into the fire and thought about all the problems and all the players involved, while his fingertips continued to smooth over her skin. With only a few words, everything had gotten more complicated. And there was no way he could protect Virginia from what would come. He realized he didn't want her hurt, not in any way. Somehow, someway, he'd begun to really care about her. He could no longer attempt to convince himself that he didn't like her, because he liked her far too much.

Admitting what was in his heart, even to himself, scared the hell out of him, but it was too big to deny.

The odds of getting away from this damn scheme unscathed had drastically diminished.

THE HEAT DISTURBED HER, covering her in thick, pulsing waves, mixing vividly with the dream. She moaned, trying to force herself awake and away from the tormenting heat. As she stirred, she curled her fingers, and felt them dig into solid muscle. She panted for breath, for recognition.

The scent of hot, excited male filled her nostrils as she sucked in a long breath. Stunned and disoriented, unable to move with any speed, she lifted her eyelids.

Her nose twitched, tickled by the dark hair of Dillon's chest, close to one flat brown nipple. Her heart skipped a beat, and she couldn't seem to get her thoughts organized other than to realize her face was pressed to Dillon's bare chest and her pelvis was perfectly aligned with his. The solid length of his erection burned against her bare belly, even through his jeans. A sweet, insistent pressure between her thighs made her shudder. Confused, she raised her head just a bit. Dillon's diamond-hard gaze immediately snared her.

Lazily, he murmured, "You're awake."

The husky rumble of his voice rubbed over her and she moaned. That was when she realized his thigh pressed against her in the most sensitive of places. Her legs straddled him and one large calloused hand anchored her naked bottom in place, his fingers pressing into her flesh, roughly caressing. Somehow the quilts were pushed low on the cot and her T-shirt had gotten shoved to her waist. His fingers dipped, sliding between her buttocks, moving down toward her mound, and she jerked in startled, excited embarrassment. *"Dillon?"*

His smile was gentle, even as those fingers slid lower, coasting over her, probing, seeking. "I like waking up with you hot and wet for me, Virginia. I like it a lot." He closed his eyes as one finger circled her, briefly pressing into her body. "Do you feel how wet you are, babe? How hot?"

A slight trembling started deep inside her. "I don't understand."

"You crawled right on top of me." As he spoke, his gaze moved over her face, lingering on her lips, then her throat, where she knew her pulse raced. He lowered his thick lashes, hiding his eyes.

She swallowed, wanting to deny his statement, but how could she when she made no effort to move away from him? She didn't want to move. She'd gone to sleep excited, wanting him so much, more than she'd ever thought it was possible to want anyone or anything. The things he did to her now, the bold way he touched her had to be forbidden. But he continued, and she didn't try to stop him.

Dillon had a strength she'd never imagined, but there was also a gentleness about him, the careful way he wielded his strength. His power was a sexy, vital part of him and she wanted him.

Unable to help herself, she squirmed. Dillon pulled his hand away, then raised his thigh a bit more, pressing hard against her while her body moved of its own volition to a rhythm she hadn't known until he showed her with a guiding hand. She gasped at the acuteness of the sensation, closing her eyes and pressing her head back.

She felt his fingers tangle in the length of her hair, moving it over his chest and shoulders. "You are so sexy."

She couldn't stand it. She shook her head, knowing it wasn't true, knowing she behaved shamefully, practically attacking Dillon in his sleep. He palmed her breast, weighing it, his fingertips rubbing roughly over her aching nipple. It pebbled hard and he lightly pinched the very tip, tormenting her. Her body become more sensitive, more alive with each small movement. She cried out.

"Do you have any idea what you do to me, Virginia?" His whispered words added to the quickening building beneath her skin. "I couldn't sleep, not with you so near at hand. And then you crawled over me, cuddling close, and you touched me, just my chest, but I felt it to my very bones."

His leg thrust higher, forcing her forward and she cried out again, arching her back to add to the delicious pressure. "Dillon..." The embarrassment was there; she'd never done anything like this before, certainly not with a man watching her so closely. And she'd never felt this way, scattered and fractured and ready to explode, *wanting* to explode. She could feel her own wetness, her heat, and she kept moving against him, seeking the sharp pleasure that kept expanding but seemed just out of reach.

Dillon lifted her breast higher and bit her nipple lightly through the cotton shirt. "I want to taste your nipples, Virginia. Hell, I want to taste all of you."

She opened her eyes, staring at him, uncomprehending. He smiled and touched her face with a trembling hand. "Let me help you, honey. You need me right now, don't you?"

"I don't know." But she did know. She wanted Dillon inside her, she wanted to know what it was to be loved by this man, even if the lovemaking was a sham. He'd lied about wanting her, lied about being attracted to her, but he wanted her now. She could feel his body moving in subtle shifts, his huge erection grinding against her belly.

"Trust me, Virginia?"

He made it a question, not an order, and she groaned, hardly able to think with his hands teasing her and showing her how to move, urging her harder against him, faster. "I do."

In the next second, Dillon flipped her onto her back, shoving her T-shirt up and over her breasts. His slim hips planted firmly between her widely spread thighs. Virginia clutched at him, stunned and excited and a little scared by the way he made her feel so out of control, so uncaring about everything in the world but the pleasure of him and the ache inside her.

Then his mouth was on her nipple while his hand held her breast high, like a sacrifice. He sucked and licked and Virginia didn't know if she could stand it, it was so exciting. She bit her lips to keep from begging, to stop herself from crying out like a wild thing. But she couldn't hold still and she writhed under him, holding his head, feeling the hollows of his cheeks as he sucked her hard, mercilessly.

The torture went on and on. He switched from one breast to the other, never quite satisfied, and she did cry, only it didn't deter him from his course. He seemed intent on driving her out of her mind, his mouth and hot tongue first light and teasing, then frightening her with sharp little nips of his teeth and rough kisses. She thrust her mound against him, rubbing and seeking, anxious to gain her own pleasure. But whenever she got close to that mystical realm of satisfaction, he would hold her hips and force her to be still, even while he continued to taste her and whisper hot, forbidden words to her.

"Damn you, Dillon." Her gasping breaths made it difficult to speak. Her words sounded high and weak.

"I want you to remember this, honey, to remember me." Now he used both hands to lightly pinch her nipples, tugging and rolling, keeping her poised, her back arched while he watched her respond with satisfaction. "I want to give you something you've never had before."

"I can't stand it...."

"Shh." He bent to lave her nipple with the very tip of his raspy tongue. "I'm not giving you a choice. Not this time."

The words sent an erotic thrill of warning down her spine. "Make love to me, damn you!"

One hand left her breast to trail down her side, then over her belly. "Not a good idea, Virginia. You want me now, but when this is all over, you're liable to hate me."

"No." She moaned as his hand slid over her, separating her slick folds, teasing her further. When she cried out, he pushed two fingers deep inside her, high and hard. Instinctively, she tried to twist away. Dillon wouldn't let her.

"Don't hide from me, Virginia. Give over to me. *Trust me.*"

How could she trust him when it seemed he only wanted to make her crazy? If he wouldn't make love to her, then why torture her so thoroughly? But she couldn't think, couldn't find a rational thought, not with his fingers stroking her, stretching her.

"Open your legs wide for me, baby. Wider...." He groaned. "That's it."

He kissed the sensitive underside of her breasts, then her ribs, counting each one. When she felt his mouth low on her belly, she held her breath, wanting to protest, but unable to speak or even think past the heightened sensation and acute painful need.

He sat back on his heels and looked at her. Using his thumbs, he spread her open, slicked up and down, sometimes dipping, then rubbing over her.

"No," she moaned, pushing his hands away and trying to cover herself. But he caught her hands and pinned them to her sides. Their gazes met and she shuddered at the hot, determined look in his eyes. "I like to see a woman touch herself, Virginia, to watch her play with her own body. But not now, not yet. Right now, I'm playing."

"Bastard." But the word was only a whisper and she didn't fight him anymore.

He released her hand and said, "Do you want me to stop?"

She trembled, then shook her head. "No."

"Then don't move. Do you understand me, Virginia?"

She didn't think she could move even if she'd wanted to. Meek compliance went against every fiber of who she was. But she knew she'd die if he stopped now, so he left her no choice. She swallowed, then turned her face away and whispered, "Yes."

"Look at me."

Again she seemed to have no choice but to obey. Her heart pounded so hard it hurt.

He trailed his fingers down her ribs, watching as she trembled from the tickling sensation that only added to her raw nerves, making her body more frenzied. Both hands stopped at the top of her thighs and he pushed, spreading her even wider.

"You look beautiful like this."

She knotted her hands in the sheets and tried to concentrate on the sight of him, his hard body, the way every muscle seemed drawn tight right now. His jaw was rigid, his eyes were burning. He traced her femininity with one rough finger, then tweaked her curls, smiling and saying, "So pretty." As he toyed with her, he asked, "Hasn't any man ever really looked at you, honey?"

She shook her head, unwilling to voice the words. Caught in a maelstrom of embarrassment and overwhelming need, she didn't dare speak for fear of what she might admit.

"Fools. I could look at you forever."

Just as he had done with her nipples, he caught her swollen bud between the very tips of his fingers and thumb. Her body bowed, lifted high, and he held her like that, lightly abrading her, stroking, pulling. If she started to close her thighs, he'd stop and rearrange her again before returning to his torment. She bit her lips and sobbed and then he bent low and she felt his breath.

Carefully now, he slid his fingers back inside her, adding a rough friction while his hot mouth closed over her, drawing gently. Everything in her tightened, the sensations all rushing to that one spot, then radiating out again in rolling waves. His lips nibbled over delicate, throbbing flesh and suckled gently while his fingers continued to fill her, and she exploded, her climax taking her by surprise as her legs tightened and her vision went blank and her body screamed in a rush of unbelievable pleasure. The power of it was so devastating, like an attack to her every nerve ending, that she honestly wondered if she'd survive—and didn't really care.

The sensation went on and on, stealing all thoughts. She wasn't even sure what it was now that Dillon did with her body and it didn't matter, as long as he continued to do it. He murmured to her, encouraged her and praised her, until she trembled and her body went utterly limp. She tugged weakly at his hair, unable to bear it a second more, hardly able to breathe.

Dillon released her with one last, leisurely lick, and she collapsed back against the bed, her skin damp with sweat, her heart pounding against her ribs, her body tingling yet almost numb. She waited for him to enter her, to gain his own pleasure. But instead she felt a gentle kiss, as soft as a breeze, over her belly, then on each breast. She was so sensitized to his touch she groaned.

Forcing her eyelids open, she saw Dillon looking down at her, his cheekbones flushed darkly, his eyes bright and burning, his lips parted and wet. He leaned over and kissed her nose, her mouth. She could taste herself and she could feel the heat of him, the repressed energy as it seemed to sizzle between their bodies. "Go to sleep, Virginia."

She blinked, barely able to keep him in focus. The firelight worked like a hypnotic drug, lulling her. "Don't you want to...?"

One side of his mouth quirked. "Oh yeah, I want to. Now, go to sleep."

When she started to speak again, he covered her mouth with his fingertips. They were still damp and scented by her body. She shuddered. "Sleep."

Though she fought it, her eyes did shut, and the last thing she remembered was Dillon gathering her close again, half pulling her over his body and covering them both with a single quilt.

Cozy and comfortable and for the first time in

her life totally, completely sexually satisfied, she must have slept like the dead. She couldn't recall stirring a single time the rest of the night, even though she'd never actually slept with a man before.

When she awoke late in the morning, her head felt muzzy and full of cotton, as if she'd drunk too much. She shifted and her body complained, sensitive in places she'd never thought about before. She winced, remembering what she'd done, what she'd let Dillon do.

How could she face him now? What would he say?

Cautiously, her eyes darting around the room, she sat up in the bed. The quiet penetrated and she gasped. No, surely he hadn't left without waking her! Not after last night. She crawled out of the bed, untangling herself from the quilts, and rushed to the door. Before she opened it she saw the note on the center of the table.

Dillon was gone.

10

THE COLD, HAZY blue-gray day could have accounted for Dillon's mood, except he knew the real reason, and it didn't sit right with him. He wasn't the sort of man who normally suffered extremes of temperament. And he wasn't the sort of man who normally felt the need to dominate a woman so completely.

Much as he missed Virginia already, he didn't look forward to facing her again. He'd slunk out of the cabin like a coward, and felt perverse satisfaction at the way she slept on undisturbed, too replete, too sated, to wake.

Last night had been the most incredible sexual experience of his life, and he hadn't even taken her.

He scratched at his rough-whiskered jaw as he pulled the truck into the parking lot of his apartment building. When he opened the door, wind whooshed past him, flapping his coat and sapping his heat. Even though the truck's heater was adequate, he felt frozen through and he worried about Virginia, wondered if he had brought in enough wood to keep her comfortable until his return. He wanted to get his business over with quickly.

He glanced at his watch as he bounded up the

apartment stairs, and saw that he had less than an hour to get to Cliff's office. He wanted to be there, to go through Virginia's files before anyone else arrived. Once it became known she wasn't going to show up, the uproar would begin, and stealing information would be even more difficult. Already his head ached, both from wanting Virginia and because he needed to leave before he got any more wrapped up in this emotional mess.

He rushed into his apartment, prodded by more than time limits. He needed to get back to Virginia, to make sure she was okay after last night. He'd pushed her, and the reward had been sweet. But would she understand?

This time, Dillon needed a hot shower to relax his stiff muscles and clear his head. With any luck at all, it would also wash away the insistent ache of unrequited lust, and the more disturbing element of overwhelming tenderness.

CLIFF WAS SITTING BEHIND his desk, poring over a stack of mail. Dillon walked in unannounced and sprawled in a plush padded chair. He waited impatiently for Cliff to finish reading. He was anxious to get this over with.

Owing to his position within the company, he had keys to every office, and as early as he'd arrived, Virginia's secretary hadn't yet been at her desk. He'd entered the inner office with no problem. He'd expected to have to weed through endless files to find any information, but he'd been surprised by a thick envelope lying in Virginia's In box. The package was without an address, blank on the outside, but tightly sealed. Without remorse, he'd opened it, and found two computer discs, along with a brief note. He'd taken the discs, together with Virginia's laptop computer, out to his car. He'd drive home, grab his truck and head back to the cabin to confront her. Anger still simmered just below the surface, where he hid it from Cliff.

He shouldn't have been surprised to discover Virginia was running her own investigation. In fact, he should have anticipated it. She took charge of everything, so why would this situation be any different? But he felt oddly nettled. She hadn't trusted him enough to confide in him. She obviously had her own suspicions about the embezzlement, but she'd kept quiet. Was it because she, too, wanted to pin the charge on Wade?

His hand fisted. He now had more than one reason to see the conniving little witch again. And he wasn't feeling overly patient.

All he needed was for Cliff to become aware of Virginia's absence, which should be any minute now. The calendar on her desk had her marked for an early meeting. But Miss Virginia Johnson was at present mostly naked and stranded in a deserted cabin. When he'd left, she was sleeping, exhausted from the pleasure he'd given her. Just the way he wanted her.

His muscles twitched in impatience. Dillon knew Cliff, knew his habits, and going through mail like a little boy hoping for a Christmas card was one of them. Sometimes it seemed as if Cliff could only believe he was really the head of the company by opening mail addressed to him as "President."

"So." Cliff looked up after laying aside the paperwork. "Have you found out anything?"

"I assume you're inquiring about your sister?"

"You're damn right. I have to know what she's up to. Do you realize she wasn't here at all yesterday? Didn't show up for work. She told her secretary she was taking the day off, but didn't say where she was going."

"Yes, I know. I went through her date book, but she didn't have anything personal written down for yesterday."

Cliff looked stunned, then very pleased by the idea. "Her date book. I never would have considered that. But maybe I should look at it, too. I mean, it's possible something that looked harmless to you could have been a meeting with a conspirator."

Dillon shook his head. He felt he had to protect Virginia's right to privacy from Cliff, even though he himself had invaded it only minutes earlier. "No. I recognized all the appointments. They were legitimate."

"Damn."

"I'm not surprised I didn't find any suspicious names there. Virginia isn't stupid or careless. If she's doing something behind your back, she certainly wouldn't make a note of it."

"Oh. I suppose that's true."

Cliff appeared to make the admission grudgingly. It probably felt too similar to a compliment for his tastes. He seemed struck by another thought. "If you knew you wouldn't find anything, why the hell look there in the first place?"

"I didn't say I wouldn't find anything. I said I wouldn't find anything concrete. What I was checking for was unaccountable time. Virginia is very organized and she strikes me as a woman who marks down all her appointments religiously. If there had been an hour or two left free, with nothing penned in—"

A knock on the door interrupted Dillon's well-rehearsed speech. Laura Neil breezed in with fresh coffee and an expression of concern. Predictably, Laura hovered near Cliff, who ignored her. He took the coffee without even a polite platitude. Dillon waited, his body in its usual negligent sprawl, but his muscles tightened in expectation. Finally, when Laura didn't leave, he saw the frown gather on Cliff's forehead.

"What is it, Ms. Neil?"

She stiffened at his tone, but otherwise showed no emotion. "Ms. Johnson's secretary says she hasn't arrived yet."

Cliff's brows rose. "Virginia's late?"

"Yes, sir. She had an appointment thirty minutes ago. Mr. Wilson from financing is downstairs waiting. He said the meeting was very important."

Without a word to Dillon, Cliff picked up his phone and punched in a number. "Damn irritant. Not like her to oversleep. What is she thinking," he muttered. Dillon, very aware of Laura listening, wanted to drive his fist into Cliff's face. He forced himself to sit still, to wait. After a moment, Cliff slammed down the phone. "She didn't answer at home, either. She's probably on her way in."

To Laura he said, "Call downstairs. Have Mr. Wilson escorted up here. And have Virginia's secretary bring me his file, right now."

Laura hesitated. "Ms. Johnson could get here any minute...."

"And I don't want to wait! Do what you're told."

Dillon heard Laura's gasp, but his biggest concern was conserving Virginia's business relations. The office door closed with a quiet click and Dillon stood. "Maybe you should think about this for a minute."

Cliff's face darkened and seconds later he flew out of his seat, cursing and pacing around the desk. He looked to be at loose ends, not quite sure what he should or shouldn't do. Dillon decided to give him a nudge in the right direction.

"For the sake of the company's reputation, why not just tell Mr. Wilson that Virginia is ill. There's a nasty flu going around. I'm sure Mr. Wilson would be willing to reschedule. No matter how important the meeting is, it can surely wait a day or two."

"You don't think I can handle things?"

The tone of Cliff's voice showed mingled concern and anger. "I think it will look bad for the company if anyone gets wind of the fact Virginia didn't show."

"Where the hell could she be?"

Surprised, Dillon narrowed his eyes and studied Cliff. "You sound almost worried."

The phone rang and Cliff, still pacing, pushed

a button so that the call came over a speaker. Virginia's secretary responded to Cliff's curt hello, saying she didn't have the keys to Virginia's desk or file cabinet and that she couldn't access the files without them. Cliff swallowed. "What's on her agenda today?"

"Three meetings here at the office and a business lunch."

"Keep trying her home number. Let me know if you reach her, or when she shows up."

"Yes, sir."

Cliff disconnected the call. After a long hesitation, he started to reach for the phone again, then cursed instead and pressed his fist against his forehead. "Yesterday and today. Something isn't right."

This wasn't quite the reaction Dillon had expected. He leaned forward on his seat. "What is it?"

Cliff drew several breaths, then dropped his hands to his sides. "Something must have happened. In all the years she's been part of this company, Virginia has never, *not once,* missed an appointment."

Dillon slowly got to his feet. This show of brotherly concern, of near panic, was rewarding in its own way, reassuring him that Virginia wasn't totally despised by her family. But it also made him wonder about his own conclusions on things. If Cliff was guilty of sabotaging Virginia's car, why would he now look so worried about her welfare?

Every time Dillon turned around, things got

more complicated. "What do you think could have happened?"

"How the hell should I know? Maybe Virginia screwed up. Maybe whoever she was working with turned on her. She was involved with someone, and I knew—*I knew*—it wouldn't turn out good. She ought to understand by now that no man pretending to be interested in her would be sincere. She should know better than to trust anyone like that."

Dillon's shoulders ached from strain. He wanted, needed, violence. The urge to hit someone or something almost overwhelmed him. "You have to give her credit for having some common sense. She wouldn't put herself at risk."

"Ha!" Cliff stabbed Dillon with an incredulous look. "She's too damn pigheaded to be cautious. She storms through life as if she alone owns it, and everyone will bow to her wishes."

Dillon thought of the way she'd writhed beneath him, pleading, crying in need, then screaming with an explosive orgasm. She hadn't been bossy then; she'd been more than eager to follow his commands.

"Damn her! What has she gotten herself into?"

Cliff's outburst cut through Dillon's heated memories. He was through playing. He needed to get back to Virginia, the sooner the better. Once they had this all wrapped up, she could deal with her brother however she wished. It wouldn't be his problem.

Summoning his most authoritative tone, the one he knew Cliff would automatically listen to, he said, "Tell Mr. Wilson that Virginia took ill.

Tell him she'll have to reschedule when she's feeling up to it. The last thing you want right now is panic running through the building. I'll go check out her house, make certain everything is secure there. I'll talk to a few people, find out who saw her last."

Cliff stepped back to lean against his desk as if he needed the support. "You think something's wrong, too, don't you?"

His face was white, and for the first time, Dillon wavered in his hatred of the man. "I have no idea. But to be on the safe side, I'll look into it." He started toward the door. "I'll get in touch with you later. Don't worry. And don't spread the news around, whatever you do."

Just as his hand closed on the doorknob, a knock sounded. He opened the door and there stood Laura with Mr. Wilson. Dillon stepped back. Cliff reached out his hand to shake Mr. Wilson's. After rapid introductions, where Dillon greeted the older man, Cliff said, "I'm sorry for the inconvenience, but Virginia is home sick today. She got taken by surprise with a case of the flu. I was hoping I could reschedule for her."

Dillon relaxed, seeing that Cliff could handle things. But as he pulled the door shut behind him, he caught the surprise on Laura's face. She stood near her desk, watching him with a worried frown. So she, too, had wondered about Virginia's well-being? Dillon nodded to her, but she caught his arm as he passed by. "She's truly okay?"

Laura was a nice woman, if a bit standoffish; it was a damn shame she wasted herself on Cliff.

Dillon patted her hand. "She's fine. Just under the weather."

"You're certain?"

His own gaze sharpened. "I'm certain. Don't give it another thought."

She didn't look convinced, but she forced a smile. "Good. I was…concerned."

Dillon stood watching her a moment longer as she seated herself behind her desk. "Ms. Johnson will appreciate your concern."

"Will you give her my regards, tell her I hope she'll be feeling better soon?"

One brow lifted. "You'll likely be seeing her before I will, Ms. Neil." Crossing his arms over his chest, he waited. He didn't like it that the secretarial pool was speculating on his relationship with Virginia. And that's what it was. Laura's concern now seemed more like curiosity.

"Oh. Of course. What was I thinking?"

"I'm sure I have no idea." With that, he left, feeling ridiculous for getting huffy with a secretary. Before much longer, everything would be settled, and when he left, all gossip would be put to rest.

His chest tightened at the thought. He knew Virginia was the type of woman he could have easily had a relationship with. She was headstrong, capable of standing up to him and anyone else. Her intelligence was appealing and her wit sharp. She was also the most sensually responsive woman he'd ever made love to, even though the lovemaking hadn't included total consummation. He knew having Virginia Johnson beneath him, open to his gaze, her soft flesh touching his, her taste on his tongue, was an experience he'd never forget. When he left her, he'd leave a part of his heart behind.

He figured he'd owe her at least that much.

HE HEARD THE SCREECH when he pulled up in front of the cabin. Given the howling of the wind and the fact that the cabin's only window and door were closed, it must have been a mighty loud screech. His blood seemed to freeze in his veins, and then his instincts kicked in.

Dillon had the door open and his body braced for any number of threats in less than a heartbeat. What he saw was Virginia, wearing nothing but his white T-shirt, frantically wielding a ratty broom and racing around the floor. "Virginia?"

Her wide, panicked eyes swung around to him, then she threw the broom and flew into his arms. An unexpected rush of emotion gripped him and he held her to him, cradling her close. But Virginia had other plans. She practically climbed his body, still yelping and babbling. He had little choice but to lift her as her frantic urgency sank in, and in the process, the T-shirt ripped. Her gaze searched the room, and Dillon, holding her secure, did the same. Then she pointed and began struggling against him again.

A big black spider, looking totally harassed by all the commotion, scuttled around the dusty floor, going first one way, then the other.

"Kill it!"

He couldn't help laughing. In the next instant, his head was ringing from the blow to his ear.

"Damn you, it's not funny. *Kill it!*"

She screamed suddenly as the spider made a haphazard, indirect line toward them. The sound caused his ears to ring yet again. He nearly dropped her when she launched into a renewed frenzy. Tightening his arms, he stepped toward the spider and, with the side of his boot, swept it out the open door. Virginia hid her face against his neck, her arms so tight around him she nearly choked him. Which was good, because it helped to keep his chuckles muffled.

Once the spider was dispatched, Dillon kicked the door closed. His earlier anger with her seemed to have evaporated as he relished the feel of her warm weight against his chest. "It's all right now, Virginia. The bug is gone."

She kept her face hidden and her grip didn't loosen at all. "It wasn't just a bug. It was a huge hairy spider and it...it *chased* me."

His lips twitched, but he sounded calm when he said, "Spiders don't have hair and they're more afraid of you than you are of them."

"Not that one. I was going through the wood, to add to the fire, and it jumped out of the pile and looked right at me. Before I could even run, it came after me. I kept pushing it away with the broom...." She shuddered and pressed her face closer, her warm breath feeling like a caress. "It wouldn't go away."

"How do you know it was looking at you?" he murmured, rubbing his cheek against the softness of her hair. "Could you see the evil glint in its eyes?"

"Yes, damn you, I could!"

He laughed, and this time she didn't hit him.

He kissed her cheek, her temple. "It's all right now. I'm sorry you were afraid. I got back as quick as I could."

She sighed, pressing even closer, not lifting her face a single inch. "I feel like an idiot, you know."

"Is that why you're still hiding?"

She nodded. "I really truly have no liking for insects."

"Really truly, huh?" Dillon glanced toward the door, smiling slightly. "I'm sure that one isn't particularly fond of you, either. It's damn cold outside."

She leaned her upper body away from him, and her cheeks were bright red. Dillon was more than a little aware of her soft thighs resting on his forearm. Beneath the T-shirt, she was naked, and his body was slowly coming alive to her scent, the feel of her in his arms.

She drew a trembling breath and his gaze dropped to her breasts, then stayed there. The neckline of the T-shirt had ripped and one soft nipple was partially visible, taunting him, making his body shudder with a violent rush of hot lust. He closed his eyes, and then Virginia's voice, strained and quavery, sounded in his ear.

"Put me down. Right now."

11

VIRGINIA FELT LIKE crying, and that infuriated her. This morning she'd been first so angry she could barely see, then so filled with remorse that she felt hollow inside. The realization that she loved Dillon had come slowly, but the thrill of it had invaded her body and soul. She knew when he left her, she'd be empty. She also knew he wouldn't, *couldn't* stay. He hadn't lied to her, hadn't led her on. He'd only made her love him, only showed her what she could have if things were just a bit different, if she were a different woman, and the knowing almost killed her.

All she could hope for now was to seduce him, to make him give her physical love, since there was no hope for emotional love. She wanted that desperately, wanted to make him feel the same things she'd felt last night. She wanted memories and awareness so that when he was gone, she'd still have a part of him. She knew her life, knew what goals she could reach and those that would never be. There would never be another man for her. Never.

So she'd intended to greet Dillon while lying on the bed, to play up to him, to be soft and feminine until he gave up and gave in. Instead, she'd raced into his arms like a lunatic, hysterical over a damn spider. Shame bit into her pride. She'd more or less forced him to hold her, when she knew she was no lightweight; she could feel his arms tremble with the strain. Never had she felt so unappealing.

"Put me down, Dillon."

He didn't answer, except that his arms tightened. Virginia peered at him and saw where he was looking. She looked down, too, and heat washed over her. Her breast was bared to his view, pushed up by the position of his arm, one nipple exposed. "Oh."

She started to reach for the shirt, to readjust it, but Dillon said, "Don't," and she went still. His eyes had turned black, filled with heat. It seemed an effortless endeavor for him to lift her even higher, enough so that his mouth could close over her nipple, and Virginia gasped. Her fingers tangled in his silky soft hair, cool from being outside, and she moaned.

He took his time, licking, sucking, rocking her slightly in his arms. He seemed in no hurry to relinquish her weight. She drew an unsteady breath. "Dillon... Put me down. I'm too heavy for you."

In answer, he raised his face and his mouth came down on hers, voracious, hungry. He bent her head back over his arm while he ate at her, thrusting his tongue possessively into her mouth, sucking her tongue into his. She felt him moving, but didn't know what was happening until her back came into contact with the cool quilts on the cot. Dillon followed her down, still kissing her, his hands busy shoving the T-shirt up. "You're not heavy, Virginia. You're perfect."

He placed biting, open-mouth kisses on her throat, her shoulder. He shoved the T-shirt out of his way and again drew on her sensitive nipples, a little roughly, shocking her, thrilling her. He moved down her ribs and belly.

"No!" Virginia caught at his hair, certain where this would lead, when what she wanted was so much more.

He lifted his face to look at her. He was so sexy, so gorgeous, she caught her breath. "No, Dillon."

His chest heaved and he leaned back to look at her, first her face, but his gaze quickly moved over her naked body. His nostrils flared, his jaw locked tight. "I want to give you pleasure, sweetheart."

The endearment touched her soul, made her feel vulnerable. She lifted her chin. "Make love to me, then."

He was shaking his head before she'd finished her request. "I can't, Virginia. You know that."

Brazenly, she cupped his heavy erection in her hand, then shuddered at the size of him. In a husky whisper not at all feigned, she taunted him, wanting to break his control. "Surely you're up to the task, Dillon."

His eyes closed and he groaned. "That's not what I mean and you know it."

"I don't care what you mean. I want you to make love to me, damn it."

"Contrary to what you believe, Virginia, you can't always have what you want."

He was set on refusing her, and she almost hated him—wished she *could* hate him. "Then leave me alone. I want everything or nothing."

"You want too much."

Disappointment choked her and she shoved him away, scrambling to her feet. She flipped her long hair over her shoulders and stalked to the kitchen, where she leaned against the counter and tried to collect herself. She would not let him know how he'd hurt her. She couldn't.

She heard the bed squeak and turned to find Dillon sprawled on his back, one forearm over his eyes. Never had she seen such an appealing sight. He'd thrown off his coat and his shirt was pulled tight over bulky, solid chest muscles and broad shoulders. His throat was tanned and she wanted to lick him there, to taste his skin. His worn jeans hugged lean hips and a tight abdomen, and his thighs, half-off the bed so that his feet rested flat on the floor, were thick and hard. In his reclining position, the tight jeans clearly defined his erection, and his size and thickness took her breath away. He was an impressive male, in every way possible.

She swallowed audibly, a little afraid of so much masculinity, but drawn to him just the same. On silent feet, she approached him, and without warning, her palm smoothed over him. He jerked, dropping his arm and eyeing her cautiously.

She straddled his lap and heard him growl. "All right, Dillon," she lied. "If you won't give me everything, then at least be fair and let me take from you what you took from me."

She felt him jerk, felt his erection move against her buttocks. His mouth opened and he sucked in air. "Virginia..."

"Shh." She caught his hands as he reached for her, and mimicking him from the previous night, she pressed them down at his sides. "Don't move."

His eyes narrowed at her familiar arrogant tone, and his smile twisted. "You haven't got the nerve."

She caught his flannel shirt in two fists and, staring him in the eye, gave a vicious jerk. Buttons flew across the room, pinging off the wall, rolling across the hardwood floor. Dillon watched her, not saying a word, but as her palms smoothed over his bare flesh, her fingers tangling in his chest hair, his eyes closed and he groaned. She shoved the shirt off his shoulders and down his arms until it caught at his elbows, where he'd tightly rolled the sleeves. She left it like that, trapping his arms, tangled above his head. His biceps bulged; his shoulders strained. She shifted, scooting on his lap, and he growled, lifting his hips.

Virginia leaned forward and lightly bit his nipple. He cursed and went still again. She licked the small wound, touching him everywhere on his upper body. His chest hair was dark, like his eyebrows and eyelashes, contrasting sharply with the sandy-colored hair on his head. She traced the bulges of muscles on his chest and shoulders, felt the silky softness of the hair in the hollows of his arms, then counted down the rippling muscles in his abdomen. She dipped her tongue into his navel and heard his harsh breathing.

"Virginia…"

"Don't you like this, Dillon?"

His words were low and guttural. "I don't think I've ever been so turned on."

She smiled and said, "Good," then nipped his erection through his jeans.

His hips lifted sharply, almost unseating her.

She nibbled on him, thrilled by his response. One hand crept lower, cradling him where he was softer, and his moans grew harsh.

In a rush, Virginia sat up and unsnapped his jeans. When she started on the zipper, he jerked his hips to the side. "Easy, baby. Slow."

Feeling how tight the material was around him, she understood the need for caution. Carefully, she eased the zipper downward, and his erection pushed free of the restriction. Heat enveloped her. His dark briefs weren't sufficient to contain him, and Virginia stood, turning her back to him and straddling one leg to tug off his boot and sock. She knew Dillon had propped himself on his elbows, that he watched her with hot eyes and a small smile. She didn't care.

Stumbling forward as the first boot came free, she steadied herself, then dropped the boot and straddled his other leg.

Dillon made a sound of approval. "I do love the view, honey."

She jerked hard and his boot slipped off. She dropped it, too, and turned to him, dusting off her hands. "Good. I love your whole body."

Fisting her hands in his jeans, she pulled them

down. Dillon lifted his hips to help her. "I've never had a woman molest me before."

"I've never been kidnapped before."

His underwear came off next, and once she tossed the briefs with his jeans, he pulled his arms free of the shirt. Virginia would have reprimanded him for that, except she was too busy ogling his body. He was all hard bone and muscle and overwhelming masculinity. He lay there on the bed, propped on his elbows, watching her at his leisure.

"You going to chicken out?"

She shook her head, but couldn't find adequate words.

"It's all right, Virginia. I won't hurt you."

She didn't quite believe him. She'd had only two lovers in her life, and neither of them had been built like him. How could he not hurt her?

"It doesn't matter." She sat on the side of the bed and wrapped one small hand around him. She couldn't circle him completely, and that fact made her heart race with mingled fear and excitement. He felt heavy and hot and incredibly hard.

He breathed heavily. "Take off your shirt, honey. If we're going to do this, let's do it right."

Virginia shook her head, then leaned forward. Her hair fanned out over his belly and thighs. Dillon groaned, his hands tangling tight in the quilt, his body rigid. When her lips slid over him, he shuddered and curled forward, one hand sliding down to her bottom, the other cupping the back of her head, guiding her. He pulled her shirt up so his hand could touch naked flesh, and

when she sucked him, opening her mouth wide
to fit him in, his fingers bit into her flesh.

"That's it." Dillon caught her up and tossed
her backward on the bed. "I can't take it, Virginia. I've wanted you too long."

"You did it to me."

Despite his arousal, he grinned. "It's just a little different."

Tears welled in her eyes, no matter how she
tried to hold them back. "Don't leave me, Dillon.
Make love to me. Please."

Their eyes locked for a long instant in time.
Dillon cursed low. "I have your laptop in my
truck. I have discs from your personal investiga-
tor, along with a note that claims unwavering evidence. It'll end today, Virginia, one way or another. And then I'll have to go. Do you
understand? I can't stay here. I..."

She opened her arms to him. "Then make love
to me now, before it's too late. Let me have what
time I can. Everything else will wait."

He hesitated only a moment more, then jerked
her legs open and positioned himself between
them. His mouth was everywhere at once, urgent
and hot. He helped her get out of the shirt, then
whispered, "Promise me you won't hate me."

"Never."

"Don't be afraid of me, either."

"I'm not." Virginia found it difficult to talk
with his naked body covering hers, moving over
her. She clutched at his hard shoulders, relishing
the feel of him, his heat and his enticing scent
that made her heady with need.

Dillon's mouth touched her cheek, and he

spoke against her skin. "You'll take me, Virginia. It'll be a snug fit, so snug I'm liable to lose my mind, but I'll make sure you enjoy it."

She shuddered, lifting her hips into the rhythmic pressure of his; neither of them seemed capable of holding still. She didn't see how it would be possible, but she wanted to feel him inside her, all of him. "Do it now."

"Oh no. You're not ready. And no way in hell am I going to rush this." His hands were at her breasts, his thumbs teasing her nipples. "I have only one condom with me."

"I have a whole box." She spoke before she thought about it, and heard Dillon's laugh.

"A whole box, huh? You really did have some high expectations for me, didn't you?"

Her body ached. Her stomach quivered, and he found the wit to joke? She pounded on his shoulders. "Dillon..."

"All right, baby." He snagged his jeans off the floor and retrieved the condom from his pocket. It was only late morning, but the cabin was still dim due to the cloudy day and the lack of windows. The firelight was mellow and golden, not bright. As Dillon opened the foil packet with his teeth, Virginia took the opportunity to touch him, to familiarize herself with his body. When she again leaned down to kiss him, mesmerized by his response to her mouth, he groaned and pushed her back on the bed.

"You're going to be the death of me, woman."

He slipped the condom on and came down over her. "Wrap your legs around me."

Nervously, anxiously, Virginia did as directed.

Dillon kept his gaze glued to hers and hooked his arms beneath her legs, lifting them even higher. She felt open and vulnerable, and in a small part of her mind, she admitted she liked it. As he started to push into her, she winced, automatically tightening her body.

He crooned to her, keeping up the subtle pressure, the slow steady rocking of his hips. "Relax, sweetheart. Don't fight me."

She tipped her face back, not wanting him to see her discomfort. Her teeth sank into her bottom lip.

Dillon released one of her legs and reached down between their bodies. With the rough pad of his thumb, he stroked her. She jumped, startled. The feeling was too acute and she tried to shy away from it.

"Shh. I'll help you, honey. Just relax." He continued plying her most sensitive flesh, determined. "Lift your breast for me."

Virginia whimpered, already in an agony of sensation.

"Do it."

With shaking hands, she cupped one breast and offered it high. His mouth clamped onto her nipple and he drew gently. "Umm."

"I can't stand it," she said, her voice high and tight.

He licked, circled her nipple. "Yes, you can."

She felt him sink a little deeper into her body. The intrusion burned, but at the same time soothed. Her body seemed to be demanding conflicting things. There was an emptiness that she wanted him to fill, and the aching pressure of him doing just that. She wanted to pull back, but she also wanted to draw him nearer.

"Dillon…"

"Just a little more. Come on, Virginia. Open up for me. You can take all of me." His thumb pressed and manipulated and she cried out. "That's it. A little more."

Her heart raced, urged on by the gentle friction of his thumb, and she gave a broken moan, lifting herself to him, hearing him groan in return, and then he thrust hard and filled her.

She recoiled, shocked, but he held her hips, keeping her still, keeping himself buried deep inside her. His chest heaved against her.

It was too much; she felt stretched too tightly, felt him much too deeply. She hadn't imagined anything like this, lovemaking out of her control, both physically and mentally. She couldn't seem to draw a breath, couldn't move because he held her so close, pinned by his body.

Slowly, she became aware of other things, of the furious gallop of Dillon's heartbeat, the strain of his muscled body over her as he struggled to remain still, his harsh, deep breathing. God she loved him, and he was hurting as much as she.

Virginia smoothed her hands down his back and kissed his shoulder. After a shaky breath, she said, "I'm okay."

He laughed, a strained sound. "I know it. But I'll admit I'm glad you realize it. I don't know how much longer I could've waited."

When he began to thrust, slow and smooth, it both hurt and tantalized. He filled her, and each deep push dragged against her sensitive flesh as surely as his thumb had. She kept her arms around his neck, her legs tight around his hips, and held on, half-afraid to let go. Dillon tangled a hand in her hair and turned her face up to his, kissing her deeply, fusing their mouths as well as their bodies. Virginia felt the first stirrings of a climax gaining quickly on her, the sizzling heat began to swirl low in her belly. *"Dillon."*

He lifted her hips in his large hands and pulled her more snugly to his body, touching her so deeply she screamed. "Yes," he groaned. "Now, baby, please, now."

He shouted, his head thrown back, every muscle in his body taut and delineated, showing his incredible strength and the wonderful way he tempered it.

Virginia watched him through a haze of pleasure and tears, loving him, missing him already. As Dillon slowly lowered himself over her, she held him close, and their heartbeats mingled. Whatever else happened, she would never regret meeting this man. And she'd never love this way again.

HE WISHED SHE'D put on some clothes. Making love to Virginia three times in as many hours hadn't satisfied his need. He felt desperate to tie her to him, to take all of her that he could while he could. Fighting his growing need for her, biting back the words he wanted so badly to say, was keeping him on edge.

But Virginia, now that she'd decided they should be lovers, held nothing back. She kept touching him, tenderly, *lovingly*, in ways he'd never been touched before, and that would set him off. Even a simple touch to his back or shoulders held special meaning when her golden eyes were smiling at him. Especially since she still wore only his shirt, even forsaking the damn quilt. She'd look at him and her lips would tremble and he'd get a hard-on every time. He wanted to drown in her scent, and had tried to do just that until she'd cried and begged and threatened to kill him if he didn't take her. He'd placed one last kiss on the warm, sweet heat of her body and then thrust into her, giving her the release she needed.

Even in bed, she was a demanding, bossy woman. She pleased him more than any woman he'd ever known or could have imagined. Leaving her would be the hardest thing he'd ever done, but he had no choice.

After a hasty lunch of sandwiches, he'd set up all her computer equipment on the rickety table and she was in the process of reading the discs. Dillon couldn't have read them at work because he didn't have the necessary password to find the files, but he was looming over her shoulder, not willing to trust her a single inch. She typed in the words *You got it.*

"That's the password?"

She laughed. "Yeah. Every time I ask Troy to do something almost impossible with computers, he says—"

"You got it."

"Right." As she spoke, she sorted through files. "Troy is my inside guy. He helped me set up some stuff on the company's computer system."

"Stuff your brother knows nothing about."

Virginia grinned at him. "Yep. You see, each computer terminal is coded. So not only does the person using the computer have a user ID, but we can track who used which computer. According to Troy's note, it got complicated tracking the embezzler because— Ah, here we go."

She read a moment, Dillon peering over her shoulder, then suddenly she stiffened. Dillon read on a moment more before he began to snicker. "Ms. Johnson," he said with mock severity. "So you were the culprit all along."

Virginia didn't think it was funny. She turned to glare at Dillon. "That bastard used my ID!"

He kissed her mouth, then didn't want to stop kissing her. She clutched at his shirt. When he pulled back, she asked, "You don't really think—"

He kissed her again, quick and hard. "Of course not." He took her hand. "Honey, did you see which terminal was used?"

Virginia glanced back at the screen. "No, I..."

Dillon waited. "It's your brother, Virginia."

"Ridiculous. Cliff would have no inkling how to do anything this elaborate." She scanned the typed words, then frowned.

"But he would surely know your user ID and all the passwords. And it was the computer in his office."

Without responding, Virginia hit a button on the keyboard and backed up several pages. "Ha!

That transaction took place during a week when Cliff was out of town."

Dillon stared thoughtfully at the screen. "You're certain?"

"I think I know what's going on in the company, thank you."

"Okay, so that only means he's working with someone, which is what I suspected all along. I had hoped, for your sake, that he wasn't involved, but it's the only thing that makes sense."

"And who would he work with?" As she spoke, she turned to face him, swiveling sideways in her chair. Seeing her naked legs and the shadow of her nipples through the T-shirt made reasoning very difficult.

Dillon knelt in front of her. "Honey, you have to realize you've collected a few enemies along the way."

"The employees respect me."

"I know that. But a lot of the management, especially the men, resent you. Don't you think it would be easy for Cliff to find a cohort if he chose to?"

"I suppose." Then she narrowed her eyes and crossed her arms under her breasts. "You told me yesterday you suspected someone. Cliff was it?"

Dillon chewed on the side of his mouth, debating what he should say to her, how he should say it. Virginia slapped a hand on the table. "Stop it! You promised to tell me everything, but now I can see you calculating! Just for once, be truthful with me."

He didn't like her tone or her attitude. Slowly,

he straightened, glaring down at her. She glared right back. He didn't want to hurt her, but she did deserve the truth. Virginia, more than any woman he knew, could handle the truth. "I think it's possible Kelsey could be involved."

She sat frozen a moment, then chuckled. "Oh, Dillon, really. Kelsey is a child."

"A child having a child? She's pregnant, she's a little desperate and from what Wade tells me she resents the constant animosity in the family."

"And you're telling me she blames me alone? Cliff's as much at fault as I am."

"Unless Cliff has convinced her otherwise. Kelsey isn't like you, babe. She's wants to be a wife and mother, not a corporate leader."

Virginia turned her face away. "I want those things, too." She shrugged, looking suddenly small and defensive, and Dillon wanted to hold her, to carry her back to bed and try to keep the world at bay. But he knew he couldn't.

"I haven't been given a lot of choices in what I want to do with my life, Dillon. The company is all I've had."

He shoved his hands deep into his jeans pockets. "Are you saying you'd give it up? That you'd walk away from it to be a wife, to have babies?"

He watched her hands curl into fists on the table, watched her shoulders stiffen. "Why couldn't a woman have both? This is a new era. A huge percentage of women work and have families."

Dillon felt the last of a small dream die away. Virginia would never leave her family's company, and he had to take care of his father in

Mexico. There was no future for them, and never had been. He'd known that from the first. He'd warned himself time and again that touching her would be a mistake. It had been nothing but foolish romanticism making him wonder if whatever she felt for him could ever be more.

Dillon pulled out the chair opposite her and straddled it. Virginia wouldn't quite meet his gaze. "I see no reason you couldn't have both, honey. If any woman could pull it off, you could. I wish you all the best, you know."

Virginia sighed. Her eyes were shiny with tears, but he pretended not to see, knowing how badly she'd hate the sign of vulnerability. She propped her head on her hand and sent him a small, shaky smile.

"I wish you the same."

They stared at each other until Dillon cleared his throat. "Well, unfortunately, the embezzlement is only part of our problem. There really was a physical threat to you. Someone got into your house using a key, and since I was with you, we'll never know what might have happened. But someone also tampered with your brake lines, and that intent can't be misconstrued. They knew what you'd be driving into, that you could have been killed. Think about it. Who would gain if you got hurt or lost your standing in the company, other than Cliff. And Lord knows that man resents your intrusion."

"I'm not intruding! I have every bit as much right to be involved as he does."

"I believe you, but does Kelsey? Does she think you might be stepping on some toes, angering her brother and in effect causing family problems?"

"You're suggesting that my family—*my brother and sister*—would deliberately do me harm."

He hated the way she looked, that obstinate set of her shoulders that told him how much he'd wounded her. He took her hand and held tight when she would have pulled away. "I just don't know, Virginia. Before today, I would have said yes, that Cliff was more than capable of such a thing."

"What happened today? Did Cliff suddenly grow a halo?"

"No. When Laura told Cliff you hadn't shown up for work, he all but panicked. He looked more concerned than I've ever seen him. In fact, I'm supposed to be looking for you right now."

"Is that right? Working a side job for Cliff?"

He started to tell her about his side job, that Cliff had hired him to keep tabs on her, but saw no point in it. She was hurting enough. "As soon as we finish reading through the results of your investigation, I can take you back, and Cliff will no doubt welcome you with open arms."

She made a face. "Don't push the bounds of reality, Dillon. If Cliff wants me kept safe, it's because he knows he can't run the company without me, regardless of the fuss he makes sometimes. That in itself proves he couldn't be the embezzler. But I suddenly have an idea who it might be."

Dillon waited, but Virginia only shook her

head. "Let's finish seeing what Troy turned up, and then we'll know."

They pulled their chairs together and continued reading the data entered in an organized way. Each case of missing money was noted, and which terminal had been used, plus the user's ID. Several of the initial thefts had been done using Wade's password. After that, things got sketchy. Small amounts were removed using Cliff's ID, Virginia's and several others. They were all taken from the same terminal. Dillon narrowed his eyes as he came to the same conclusion as Virginia.

"The necessary info could have been stolen from Cliff. Only the people with highest security clearance would have had access to all those codes."

Virginia nodded. "I keep my important files locked up, but Cliff isn't nearly as responsible. It's possible that someone with access to his office could have found the codes, without knowing that the terminals were also monitored."

"Laura Neil." Dillon stared at Virginia as so many things started to take shape in his mind. "It makes sense. The original thefts were blamed on Wade, and he used to be involved with her before he met Kelsey."

"And Cliff got her on the rebound. I hate to say it, but he hasn't treated her well. She knows that we argued about her, that I tried to convince Cliff to have her transferred if he was going to become involved with her. But he refused and I let it go. Now it appears their affair is over, but she's in the awkward position of still being his secretary."

Dillon leaned back in the chair and rubbed his eyes. "I felt sorry for her today, Cliff was so indifferent to her. She acts like she's still very hung up on him."

"'Acts' being the operative word. It wouldn't do for her to show she despised him. If that happened, she might get fired, and that would put an end to her skimming money."

"Damn, I can't believe I overlooked her. She just seemed so...pathetic."

Virginia made a rude sound. "Face it. You overlooked her because she's female and you wanted to blame Cliff."

With a raised brow, Dillon admitted, "That, too."

"We have to get out of here. I need a phone so I can call Troy. He can put a personal audit on Laura. We should be able to figure out if the money has shown up in her accounts. Plus he knows her. Any fancy new cars or expensive vacations might prove interesting."

"Troy can access her accounts?"

"He's a top-notch hacker, which is the main reason I keep him around and pay him a damn good wage. I want him working for me, not against me."

Virginia stood, then looked at Dillon expectantly. "I'll need my clothes."

Once again, his gaze skimmed her body; he relished the sight of her, the lush curves and feminine roundness. "Not yet. I have a cellular in the truck. Let me get it and you can call Troy from here."

"Why not just go back to my place and call?"

With his hands on her shoulders, Dillon bent low to give her a direct look. "Because someone wanted to hurt you, which you seem to keep forgetting. I'm not taking any chances with your safety. Once I find out if it really was Laura, then we can contact the police and go from there."

He could tell Virginia wanted to argue, but he ignored her protests and went out to the truck. She could make her calls, but there was no way he would let her put herself at risk. He might not always be around to protect her, to cushion her from the world and her own prickly pride, but he was here now, and he wanted her to know how important she was to him. He couldn't tell her, but he could try to show her.

VIRGINIA HUNG UP the phone. It was nearing six o'clock and Troy had been diligently applying his computer expertise for the past several hours. She turned to Dillon, feeling equally relieved and sad. They had the information they needed, and that was a relief, but it also meant their time alone was over. Dillon would take her from the cabin and the real world would intrude. She felt the loss like a physical blow.

"What did he find out?"

Virginia had been jotting down all Troy said, and now she flipped the piece of paper toward Dillon. "Laura had enough of the deposits in her accounts, in the same amounts as the missing funds, to prove her guilt. Stupid, really, but I suppose she thought the amounts were small enough not to matter. I mean, a couple of hundred here and there is really not all that noticeable when taken from so many different sources. Troy said she also has her house for sale."

"The amounts might have been small, but they really added up." Dillon stood and stretched his shoulders. "I guess that cinches it."

"If it's okay with you, I'd like to go by the office and get all the files on this together. We can notify the police in the morning from my house."

She watched him, hoping he wouldn't argue. They should probably move tonight, but she was so tired, and she hoped to have one more night alone with Dillon. His sad smile showed he had the same thought. Though they'd made love for hours while waiting for news, it hadn't been enough. Virginia didn't think a lifetime would be enough, but every day was precious.

"Tomorrow is fine," he told her softly.

He stepped close and kissed her, holding her face between his large warm hands and lingering until she thought she might beg him to stay at the cabin with her. But she knew that couldn't be. According to Dillon, Cliff was worried, and she could only imagine how relieved Wade would be to know he was in the clear. Those people deserved to be told as soon as possible.

Dillon brought Virginia's clothes in from the truck and laid them by the fire to warm while she showered. A half hour later, they were on the way home.

12

DILLON KNEW SOMETHING was wrong the second the elevator opened onto the floor. He couldn't exactly explain his unease to Virginia, because it wasn't anything concrete, just a gut reaction that told him she was in danger.

She'd been holding his hand since they left the truck. No woman had ever held his hand, not even when he was a kid. He never had a mother, and the endless string of women his father had brought around weren't interested in a little boy. The gesture now seemed sweet and almost protective. He didn't want her to let go. But he had to keep her safe.

"I want you to wait downstairs with the night-shift guard."

Virginia raised her brows. "Why? Cliff is surely gone for the night, so you won't get a chance to confront him, if that was your thought."

She was too astute for own damn good. "I would have done that. In fact, I'd like to break his damn nose. But right now I have other concerns." He hesitated a moment, then admitted, "Something doesn't feel right."

Smiling, Virginia tugged on his hand and started him down the hallway to Cliff's office.

"Let me guess. You expect to find Laura Neil brandishing a bazooka and threatening the masses?"

Dillon pulled her up short and shoved her behind him, staring down the dim hallway. "Now who's underestimating a woman?" He nodded toward Cliff's office and they both saw that a light was on, shining dully through the etched window in the door. The entire floor should have been shut down and locked for the night.

Virginia stared. "Well, hell. What is that brother of mine up to now?"

"Shh. Not another word out of you or I'll lock you in a closet." When she started to protest, he said, "I mean it, Virginia. I have the keys in my pocket, so don't test me."

Luckily for his peace of mind, she didn't argue. Dillon pressed her down on the floor, in the shadows of a large decorative plant. "Stay here. I'm going to see what's going on." He narrowed his gaze on her. "Don't move."

Glaring, Virginia gave him a mock salute. He answered by kissing her. "I couldn't stand it if anything happened to you, honey." As he crept away, he could feel Virginia's eyes on his back.

The door to Cliff's outer office opened silently. Dillon peered in, saw the inner office was the one brightly lit and slid through the doorway. As he moved along the wall, nearing the inside door, he could hear the muffled tones of people speaking. Rather than burst in, he took his time, listening and assessing the situation.

It didn't take long to figure out that Laura had already guessed her game was over. Cliff feebly tried to claim he loved her, gaining even more of Dillon's disdain, but Laura only laughed. Her voice overrode Cliff's panicked one.

"You always were a sniveling bastard, Cliff. You deserve anything I do to you."

"I thought you cared about me."

Her words took on a hard edge. "Yes, maybe at first. When Wade dropped me, I was content to set him up, to make him pay. You'd fired him, and that was enough punishment. But your sister insisted on investigating everything. She wanted to ruin all my plans, including my plans for you."

"Virginia had nothing to do with me and you."

"You're so naive, Cliff. You pretended to care about me, and I stupidly thought you'd marry me. I knew the only hindrance would be Virginia. She'd go to any lengths to protect this damn company, and that means she'd keep digging about the missing money until she finally caught up to me."

"You did something to her?"

There was indifference in Laura's tone. "I didn't really intend to hurt her, just distract her from the investigation. I figured if she had to worry about her own life, she wouldn't have time to stick her nose into the business."

Dillon heard Cliff clear his throat. He could almost taste the man's fear and assumed Laura had a gun trained on him. Cliff's voice shook when he spoke.

"But then I lost interest in you, so that changed everything?"

"Not really. I'd already realized that even if you married me, it wouldn't have mattered. Eventually Virginia would have succeeded in totally discrediting you. She's the ruling factor in this company, not you. So I decided to take one more hefty sum and get out. It was stupid of you to show up here tonight, Cliff."

"I was worried about my sister, damn you."

"Hmm. And that surprises me. I thought the two of you hated each other. Or were you worried because you know without Virginia, you'd fail completely?"

For the first time, Cliff sounded angry. "*Bitch.* She's my sister, and regardless of our differences, I love her. This damn company has nothing to do with it."

Dillon sensed Virginia's presence even before she touched his arm. He turned. She stood in the darkness right behind him, tears glimmering in her eyes. He wanted to curse, wanted to throttle her and lock her away someplace safe, but he couldn't do a damn thing. Any noise at all would distract Laura, and after Cliff's melodramatic confession, he really didn't want to see the man shot.

Dillon raised a finger to his lips as Laura again spoke.

"I do wonder where your errant sister is."

"If you've hurt her, Laura, I'll kill you."

That caused a burst of hilarity. "I'm the one with the gun, Cliff. And believe me, I wouldn't mind putting a bullet through your cold heart. But first, finish transferring the funds as I told you. We've done enough talking."

There was the almost silent pecking of the keyboard, and then Cliff said wearily, "It's done."

"Excellent. Now, stand up and come over here."

"You can't shoot me in the office, Laura. The night guards would hear. And you know, since hiring the new security manager, the men working are more than capable."

"Shut up while I think."

"You know why I grew tired of you so quickly, Laura?"

"Shut up."

"Probably the same reason Sanders did. You play the role of lapdog to perfection. You can complain about my sister all you like, but at least she's an intelligent woman. She provides conversation and wit, not just babbling."

"Shut up, damn you!"

"All I got from you was blind adoration, and at times it almost made me sick."

Laura lost her temper, screeching in rage, and that's when Dillon threw open the door. Laura whirled, getting off a wild shot that missed Dillon as he rolled across the floor. Cliff ran to the outer office, almost knocking Virginia down as she stuck her head in the doorway. Dillon effectively tackled Laura, gripping her wrist and squeezing until she dropped the gun. Virginia, much to his dismay, ran in and picked up the weapon. Laura still fought him, scratching his neck and the side of his face, kicking her long legs wildly.

When Virginia realized Dillon planned to do no more than hold her, regardless of how she injured him, she knelt by Laura's head and whispered, "Put one more mark on him, and you'll have me to deal with."

There was enough venom in her tone to make Laura go completely still. Dillon grinned at Virginia, then came to his feet, holding Laura's wrists in one hand.

Security guards rushed in, guns drawn, and they took control of Laura. Dillon removed the automatic weapon from Virginia's hand, giving her a chiding glance. "You were supposed to stay in the hall, safe."

Before she could answer, Cliff began a hysterical recitation of the events. Dillon listened with half an ear, most of his attention on Virginia, who looked pale. The guards handcuffed Laura and led her to the outer office. The police had been called and would arrive shortly.

"It's really over, isn't it?"

Huge tears welled in her eyes and Dillon had difficulty swallowing. "Don't do this, baby. You're killing me."

"I love you, you know."

He closed his eyes, drawing a shuddering breath. "I have to leave now. My father's waiting for me in Mexico. Nothing will change that."

Cliff sidled up to them and clamped a hand on Virginia's arm. "Oh, this is rich. I'm here, almost getting shot, and you've obviously been off whooping it up with an employee!"

Dillon gave Virginia an apologetic look, his eyes never leaving her face, and with his left hand, socked Cliff right in the nose. The smaller man went down like a stone.

His hand, no longer fisted, cupped her face. "If you ever need me, honey, just let me know."

Her expression changed, became almost desperate. "No, you can't leave now. I won't allow it."

Her panic twisted his insides. "It's better if I don't get tangled up with the police. You can handle things."

Cliff writhed on the floor next to them, holding his bloody nose and cursing.

"Dillon—"

He leaned forward and kissed her, a kiss of tenderness and regret. "I love you, Virginia." The tears spilled over and he groaned in genuine agony. "Shh. God, don't cry, Virginia. If I could change things, I swear I would."

Her chin lifted. "I'm glad you kidnapped me."

He managed a smile at her false bravado. "I have a feeling it'll always be my fondest memory." He touched her cheek one more time, then turned to go. As he passed through the outer doorway, he heard Virginia bark, "Oh, come on, Cliff, get up. We have to take care of this mess."

Dillon smiled. She would be okay. She didn't need him. The truth was, he needed her. She'd filled him up, made him whole and gave credence to his beliefs about life and love and reality. His gut cramped painfully, more so with every step he took, and he decided he might as well get used to the feeling. Because he knew that for the rest of his life, he would feel empty.

He figured it was no more than he deserved.

A month later

"WADE SAYS HE GOT a hefty promotion, along with a bonus."

Dill Sr. laughed. "A little retribution to ease the guilt?"

"I suppose. Virginia was responsible for the promotion. Cliff, believe it or not, provided the bonus as a wedding present, and from what Wade said, it was a large one."

"Good for him. Doesn't hurt to start off a marriage financially sound. True love will take you only so far."

Dillon stared at his coffee for long moments, lost in thought, then finally tipped the cup to his mouth and took a large gulp. The bitter taste suited him just fine on this hot, dusty morning. He put Wade's letter aside.

Staring at his father, seeing a glimmer of amusement in the dark eyes so like his own, he said, "Virginia is handing over a lot of the control to Cliff. According to Wade, Cliff's learned his lesson."

"So why the long face, then? You know, I'm getting damn tired of watching you brood."

His father grinned when he said it, had been grinning since the moment Dillon walked back in from his week-long buying trip a few hours earlier. "I'm not brooding. There's just something I don't understand." He ignored the toast his father pushed toward him and concentrated on his coffee, instead. "According to Wade, resolving the problems in the company has brought Virginia and her family closer together. Virginia even offered to sell out to Cliff, but he wouldn't take her offer. He says he needs her guidance and input until he learns how to run things on his own. Kelsey has gotten involved, too, along with Wade, so they're lending a helping hand."

"Sounds like a real family-run organization."

"I suppose. But I can't see Virginia offering to sell out. That company means too much to her. It's her whole life. I'm afraid something's not right."

"You're just afraid you made a damn fool mistake, that's all. I keep telling you, you should go back for her. You find a woman like that, you don't just let her go."

Dillon had heard it endless times. For weeks, his father had picked his brain for every detail. Dillon hadn't admitted to loving Virginia, fearing his father would suffer guilt, rightfully assuming that Dillon stayed only because his father needed him.

"Tell me again what she looks like."

"Dad..." Talking about Virginia, remembering, hurt like hell.

"Long red hair, right? Round in all the right places."

"Yeah." Dillon grinned despite himself. "And soft and sexy, but so mule headed she scares most men away."

"Humph. Not my son."

Dillon grunted at his father's misplaced pride. "She's strong. And a fighter."

"A woman like that'd make a damn good wife and mother."

Thinking of Virginia that way tormented Dillon. He could so easily see her with a baby in her arms and a corporate report on her desk. She'd make beautiful babies, with tempers as fiery as her own. And between the two of them, their children would never feel alone or afraid.

But it wouldn't happen. Dillon had told her that if she ever needed him to let him know. She could easily have gotten his address from Wade, but he hadn't heard from her. She'd gotten on with her life, just as he'd told her to do, but the reminder of what he'd lost ate at him day in and day out.

He finished off his coffee and shoved back his chair. "I have a fence to repair today and the vet's coming to check over the new mares I bought. I gotta get out of here."

As Dillon started to stand, his head swam. He sank back into his seat, cursing. His father grinned.

Dillon couldn't get sick now, because that would give him too much free time to think about Virginia. Since returning to the ranch, he'd filled his days with the hardest physical labor, working from sunrise to sundown. His nights were the worst; he filled them with endless paperwork and expansion plans. None of it helped. Virginia was never far from his thoughts.

He looked at his father, but his face wouldn't come into focus. "What the hell is going on?"

He heard a door open and Virginia stepped into the kitchen. Dillon blinked, not sure he was seeing right, wondering if he'd only imagined her because he missed her so damn bad. He lifted a heavy hand toward her and she dropped to her knees by his chair. "I love you, Dillon."

"God." He must be dreaming. "You can't be here."

"Oh, I'm here all right. It's payback time. You told me to let you know if I needed you. Well, I do. But I need you forever, not just for a little while. You didn't come to me, so I'm taking you."

He could feel himself fading. "What did you do?"

"I drugged your coffee."

And his father, through his chuckles said, "Damn, but she learned from a master, didn't she?"

As Dillon started to slump, Dill Sr. called out, "Come and give the lady a hand, boys. My son is no lightweight."

Virginia, a touch of worry in her tone, said, "Thank you, sir, I wouldn't want him to get hurt."

"Call me Dad. We're going to be related, after all."

And Dillon smiled groggily.

DILLON AWOKE NAKED. He opened his eyes slowly, looking around. He felt silk sheets beneath him, nothing over him. At least he'd had the decency to leave Virginia in her lingerie, providing her a bit of modesty. He'd even covered her with a quilt. Of course, Virginia wouldn't show such consideration, the witch. He chuckled.

This...*palace* was nothing compared with the cabin he'd taken her to. There was champagne chilling in a bucket of ice beside the bed and a gas fireplace blazed brightly. He started to sit up, and that's when he realized his hands were tied. He looked over his shoulder. A soft, woven velvet rope was knotted around his wrists and then looped through a scrolled newel post on the back of the bed. His body stirred, his loins tightened.

Virginia opened a door and walked in, her bare feet sinking into the thick carpet. "You're awake!"

He tugged on the ropes, working up a believable frown. He didn't want to spoil her fun. "Was this necessary?"

Perching on the side of the bed by his hip, she surveyed his naked body. Her gaze lingering on his erection. "What have you been thinking about, Dillon?"

"About making love to you right now."

Her eyes brightened and her cheeks flushed. "Yes, well… I do believe we have a few things to get straight first."

"Take off your robe."

She made an exasperated face at him. "Really, Dillon. I'm the one in charge right now. That's why you're tied down. You have a tendency to run roughshod over me."

"You like it. Now, take off the robe."

She hesitated a moment, then shrugged. "Suit yourself." The gold satin robe slid down her shoulders to pool at her hips. She stood, then pushed it aside. Dillon stared at her lush body. "I missed you something terrible, baby."

She lay down beside him, one hand resting on his taut stomach, her head on his chest. "Not as bad as I missed you. Every day, I wanted to call you, to insist you come back to me. But you were so final when you left, and it…it hurt too much to think you might turn me away again."

"I never did that, honey."

"I know. Wade told me that you'd never leave your father. He said he thought you wanted to be with me, but that your loyalty would keep you in Mexico."

Dillon kissed the top of her head, carefully testing the strength of his restraints. He didn't know how much longer he'd be able to wait and let her lead the way. "I knew you wouldn't leave the company, and I couldn't leave Dad. I'm all he has, Virginia."

"I understand. But the company doesn't mean that much to me. I thought it did, because it was all I had. But then I had you, and I knew nothing else mattered as much."

"You offered to sell your share of the company to Cliff so you could come back to Mexico with me."

She surprised him by leaning up and shaking her head. "No. I can't see me living in Mexico *and*," she said when he started to object, her expression stern, "you will let me finish. I'm not good at roughing it, Dillon."

He glanced around at his surroundings. "So I can see."

"Well, I'm sorry, but being chased by huge nasty spiders and having my feet freeze aren't memorable moments."

He narrowed his eyes. "And what about the rest of it?"

"The stuff women dream of."

He grinned.

"Kelsey will give birth in a few months, and Cliff still needs me to guide him, at least until he catches on a little better. I'm going to be a consultant for him."

"I see."

"Living in Mexico would really complicate things, put me too far out of reach."

Dillon fought back his rising anger. "You're not leaving me again, Virginia, so you can forget it."

She kissed him, long and deep, her body moving over his, her hands exploring. Finally she lifted her head, and Dillon felt sharp frustration.

"Your father and I have it all worked out."

He groaned. "You've been plotting with my father?"

"We talked quite a bit while you were out of town. He wants to live with his housekeeper."

"With Maria?" Dillon couldn't quite take it in. Maria was a wonderful person, ten years younger than his father, and not at all his type.

Virginia laughed. "They're in love. They want to get a small house and take care of each other. I thought we'd hire someone to check up on them twice weekly, just to make certain they're doing okay." Her brows drew together in a frown. "As big and powerful as your father seems, he's still old enough to need a little help, I think."

Dillon chuckled. His father was six feet two inches tall, weighed almost as much as Dillon and still had a commanding air about him. "Lately he's had a few health problems, but he doesn't like to admit it. Come to think of it, Maria is the only one he lets pamper him. Now I know why."

Virginia toyed with the hair on Dillon's chest, not quite meeting his eyes. "Don't get mad, okay?"

He stilled. "What did you do?"

"I bought a ranch." She spoke quickly, giving away her uncharacteristic nervousness. "It's a little bigger than the one you have in Mexico— Damn it, Dillon, stop shaking your head at me! It's not like it's a bribe or anything. Once you sell your ranch, you can pay me half on it, okay?"

"No, it's not okay." He tugged at his restraints, but stilled when she huffed out a curse.

She sat up, her legs astride his hips, her arms crossed under her bare breasts. "This is why I tied you down! You're so damn stubborn!"

He choked on that, distracted from the enticing view of her body. "Me? You think *I'm* stubborn?"

"Yes! I love you. I want us to be together. I'm willing to let Cliff run the company now, but I can't let him ruin it, and I can't just sit idle. So I'm starting my own business. The ranch and the business property I just bought are in the States, not that far from your father, but closer to my family so I can check up on Cliff and we can visit with Wade and Kelsey and the baby when it gets here."

"Virginia—"

"You'll love the area, Dillon, I promise. It's in New Mexico, due north of Albuquerque, and the ranch house is huge and the land is beautiful and the people who owned it raised horses but then they had to sell and…well, it's perfect…for us."

Dillon dropped his head back and laughed. She could make him nuts with her take-charge attitude, but he'd missed her so much. "All right. I'll look at the ranch. But I'm paying you back for all of it. I'm not going to live off your money, Virginia." He didn't want her ever to wonder at his motives, not when so many men had tried to use her.

She snorted. "Then I won't live off yours, so if you won't let me pay half for the ranch, I can't live there. I guess that leaves us at an impasse."

Quietly, he studied her rigid posture and mutinous expression. He knew she felt free to be so bossy, given that he was tied down. He decided to put an end to that before things got out of hand. They might as well start things off right. "Honey, move for a minute."

She looked hurt first, then angry, as she scuttled off his abdomen to stand beside the bed. Dillon laced his fingers together tightly, flexed his arms and broke the small spindle off the back of the bed. Virginia stood there, her eyes wide, and gaped at him as he loosened the rope and tossed it aside. He turned to her with a narrowed gaze. "Now."

She launched herself at him, knocking him back on the bed and sprawling over him. Her hands tangled in his hair and she held his face still while she kissed him all over, his nose, his chin, his eyes. "I love you, Dillon. Please, say you'll marry me. Let's have babies and a home and grow old together."

He locked his arms around her and rolled her beneath him. She was so beautiful to him, so determined and gutsy and proud. Her hair fanned out over the pillows, wild and tangled and as fiery as the hot temper he adored. Her cheeks were flushed, but her golden eyes seemed filled with doubt, and he wouldn't allow it. He didn't like her being humble, not when she had arrogance and bravado down to a fine art. "I love you," he growled, tightening his hold. "One way or another, I'm never letting you go, so you might as well get used to it."

She grinned as he kissed her, tears seeping from her eyes. When Dillon lifted his head, he said, "Everything will work out, Virginia. I really do love you."

"I love you, too." She spoke softly, almost shyly, peeking up at him. "And I adore your father. He made me promise we'd have some babies right off." Her gaze flicked up to his face, then away again.

Dillon kissed her nose. "I'm willing."

"I told him if he got rid of that horrid tattoo of a naked lady on his arm, he could be a surrogate grandfather to Kelsey's baby, too."

Astonished and momentarily distracted from his need, Dillon croaked, "You're kidding, right?" When she just blinked up at him, he said, "You tried telling my father what to do?"

She snorted. "I didn't try. I told him. He can't possibly be around children with that...*thing* on his arm. It's obscene." She shuddered. "Do you know where he got that? He told me the most outrageous story—"

Dillon kissed her quiet, the love inside him almost more than he could bear. She was incredible. No wonder his father was so anxious to see him married to Virginia. He couldn't think of another woman who'd ever dared to try to boss his father. More than anything, Dill Sr. respected courage, and Virginia had that in spades.

He'd also loved being a father, despite his claims of incompetence. Dillon had no doubt his father would make an excellent grandpa, but he was pleased to let his dad begin with Wade's baby. He could start all over again with the lectures on family bonds and loyalty, and this time, he'd have Dillon and Virginia to help him.

Dillon decided he'd make a show of sizing up the ranch, just to keep Virginia from getting the upper hand. But in truth, he didn't care two cents for where he lived, as long as she lived there with him. Having her for a wife, having children with her, sounded as close to perfection as he was ever likely to get.

Then Virginia moaned softly for him, accepting him as he slowly joined his body to hers, and he knew he'd already reached perfection. She was a bossy little woman, but she was his, and it couldn't get any better than that.

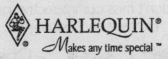

MEN *at* WORK

All work and no play?
Not these men!

July 1998

MACKENZIE'S LADY by Dallas Schulze

Undercover agent Mackenzie Donahue's
lazy smile and deep blue eyes were his best
weapons. But after rescuing—and kissing!—
damsel in distress Holly Reynolds, how could
he betray her by spying on her brother?

August 1998

MISS LIZ'S PASSION by Sherryl Woods

Todd Lewis could put up a building with ease,
but quailed at the sight of a classroom! Still,
Liz Gentry, his son's teacher, was no battle-ax,
and soon Todd started planning some
extracurricular activities of his own....

September 1998

A CLASSIC ENCOUNTER
by Emilie Richards

Doctor Chris Matthews was intelligent, sexy
and *very* good with his hands—which made
him all the more dangerous to single mom
Lizette St. Hilaire. So how long could she
resist Chris's special brand of TLC?

Available at your favorite retail outlet!

MEN AT WORK™

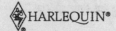 

Look us up on-line at: http://www.romance.net   PMAW2

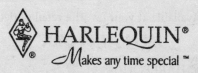

COMING NEXT MONTH

#701 IN HOT PURSUIT Patricia Ryan
Hero for Hire

Of all the bodyguard assignments Roman Fitzpatrick had endured, this was the hardest. He had to protect Summer Love; she didn't want protection. He blamed gossip-hungry journalists for destroying his police career; she was a flighty gossip columnist. He was a man; she was a woman....

#702 LOVE YOU FOREVER Janice Kaiser
The Cowboy Club

The moment Erica Ross walked into the Cowboy Club her life changed. The legendary Western place oozed romance and cowboys. And tall, sexy, strapping Clay McCormick was exactly the kind of man she needed. But could it last *forever*?

#703 STILL HITCHED, COWBOY Leandra Logan
Mail Order Men

Matt Colter advertised for the woman of his dreams in *Texas Men* magazine. What he got was a nightmare! A blond socialite fiancée, Tiffany—and a beautiful brunette ex-wife, Jenna, who wasn't *exactly* an ex. This cowboy was still hitched, still in love...and he had to follow his heart!

#704 A TOUCH OF BLACK VELVET Carrie Alexander
Blaze

Alec Danielli *knew* that being Lacey Longwood's protector would sorely test him. She was the Black Velvet vixen, Madame X—*every* man's fantasy. And he couldn't touch her....

AVAILABLE NOW: